THE SURPRISE CHRISTMAS BRIDE

VICTORIAN ROMANCE

CHARITY MCCOLL

PUREREAD.COM

CONTENTS

WAKING AS A STRANGER

*W*hy was it so hot? The heat was like a violent force, enveloping her in a fiery sheath from which she could not free herself. Try as she might, her legs would not move and she could not run away from the intensity. Encased in darkness, trapped in the blanketing heat, Gabriella could do nothing to alleviate the agony. And the noise, a great, boisterous tumult of sounds that she could not decipher noises that she had not heard before, combined with the screams of people who were invisible to her. The noise was overwhelming, joining with the terrible heat to cut off her senses so that she could neither see nor hear, only smell the dreadful malodorous aroma of burning.

"There, there, Madame, it's just the dreams coming again," a young and soothing voice somehow managed to break open a crack in the wall that surrounded her, bringing in the fragrance of soap and the comforting smell of hot coffee.

Gabriella opened her eyes. How strange that she had found it so difficult, nay, impossible to open them just moments before. A smiling visage framed in a mob cap that revealed nothing but a friendly face with warm brown eyes and a vivid fluff of reddish-brown curls on the forehead was looking down at her.

"We have been hoping that you would awaken," the voice said. "Yesterday, we thought it would be soon, so we wanted to make sure one of us was here when you awoke. We thought you might be frightened if you woke up and you were alone."

"Where am I?" Gabriella asked curiously. Tapestried bed curtains, pushed back so that the young woman could attend to her, revealed an elegant workmanship that was unfamiliar to her. This was not her bed. She had never slept in such a bed, nor had she slept upon such a mattress, or beneath such soft linens, or put her head upon such a mound of pillows. This was the bed of a dream, not of the reality of her home on the outskirts of London where the row of houses, each one identical to the next, provided habitation for the ordinary men and women who labored in the city and came home each day, weary but proud of their employment and their honest means.

"Why, you're in your home, of course, Your Grace," the girl said, her expression turning from geniality to concern. "And a magnificent home it is, the finest in all of Lancashire."

"Lancashire! I don't live in Lancashire. I've never been to Lancashire. I live outside London."

The girl's hand reached out to touch Gabriella's forehead. "A touch of fever," she pronounced, sounding relieved. "No doubt it's startled you a bit and given you a bit of . . ." she didn't finish the sentence. "Let's get some food into you and I am sure that you'll be right as rain in no time. The Doctor says that once you're back to a normal routine, he's confident that you'll mend."

"Doctor?" Doctors were frightfully expensive. No one, no matter how ill, could afford a doctor, preferring instead to go to old Maudie Winslow, who was so knowledgeable about herbs that she could boil up a tonic in no time that would do what a doctor could do and at no cost. "Why have I been to the doctor?"

"'Tis the doctor who's been to you, of course," the girl said, dumbfounded at the notion that the Lady Wibberley would ever go to the doctor as if she were one of the common folk, with their common maladies. The doctor came to her. "He's been every day, and we're finally starting to see some improvement. Not everything yet," she added hastily. "But 'twill come, he's sure of that. Rest and no excitement, he says, that's what you need. Let's hope he lets up on the no excitement rule, as I'm sure the Christmas party will be exciting. It always is."

"Who are you?"

"Of course, you wouldn't know me," the girl said. "I'm Bessie Trask. Beg pardon for forgetting that; you've been in what they call an unconscious state for weeks. His Grace hired me and Louisa to nurse you so that you would have constant care. Louisa will be here overnight to see to you."

"Why should I need anyone to care for me? I must get up and tend to my duties; Mother will wonder why I am so late abed."

"Madame, you have a fever and it's addled your wits a bit," the girl called Bessie said with certainty. "And no wonder. You've been in bed all this while after the accident. Now, let's not talk of such unpleasantness. I will help you to sit up and then I shall feed you some of Mrs. Pomeroy's excellent broth. That and a nice, hot cup of coffee will have you feeling better. You've been without nourishment so long, 'tis no surprise that you're a bit confused. Now you just sit up, like this, that's it, all those nice pillows behind you."

Gabriella felt dizzy as Bessie helped to raise her so that she was upright against the pillows. Weakly, she leaned back against them, worn out by the exertion. What on earth was the matter with her? She was a strong young woman midway between twenty and thirty and she had never been sick a day in her life.

"Not to fear, Madame," Bessie assured her. "Now that you're sitting up instead of laying down, you'll soon feel stronger. Every day, I warrant. Here, take a sip of coffee, that'll warm you. 'Tis a damp day, to be sure. And sure damp 'twill turn to snow."

Gabriella raised her hand to take the cup and then gasped.

"Whose ring is that?" she asked in a frightened whisper. She'd hang from the gallows for stealing such a gem and no one would believe her tale that she had no idea how it came to be on her finger. It was a gleaming band of gold with what looked to be diamonds set into the metal. Gabriella owned no jewelry and had certainly never worn anything of this value before. Perhaps it was an imitation, she thought hopefully. But why, in that case, was it on the finger that would, if she were a married woman, bear a wedding band.

"Why, 'tis yours, to be sure. It's been on your hand since you took to your bed, and I'm surprised that it hasn't fallen off your finger. You've lost a bit of weight, to be sure, but if you take your meals regularly, you'll be back to yourself in no time, the Doctor says."

"Why should I have a wedding ring on my finger? I am not married." There was no time for courtship; her parents were older and her mother, formerly a nurse, was in failing health and needed Gabriella to care for her. She would have liked to marry and have children, but it seemed unlikely that such a thing would ever happen at her age. Women of twenty-five did not suddenly captivate a man and entertain proposals of marriage.

"I should think it very odd if the Duke of Lancashire married a woman and neglected to give her a wedding ring," Bessie chuckled at the thought. "His Grace comes in every day to visit you."

"Here," Gabriella said, taking the ring from her finger. It was very loose and came free without effort. "Give it to him. I don't know whose ring it is but it is assuredly not mine."

"But Madame," Bessie protested. "'Tis certainly yours. Who's else would it be?"

"I have no idea but it is not mine," Gabriella insisted. She did not know what was about, but she was not going to end up in Newgate Prison as a thief. Sentences were harsh for thieves who stole from their betters. The Burchells might be poor folk, but they were honest.

"Let's just not fuss over it now, shall we," Bessie suggested, desperation in her voice as she held the ring that the Duchess had discarded.

"I hear voices, that's a promising sound," a male voice entered, accompanied by the footsteps of someone who was no stranger to the room.

Bessie turned around. "Your Grace! An early Christmas miracle!" she said, relief vivid in her voice. "Her Ladyship has awakened, and she's having a nice cup of coffee. Only her ring is a bit loose and for safe keeping, she would like you to take it."

Michael Wibberley, Duke of Lancashire did not disguise his puzzlement as he accepted the ring. "I do not believe this ring has ever left your finger since our wedding day," he said in bemusement. "You chose the setting yourself."

"I have never seen that ring before," Gabriella declared. "I am not a thief and I will not wear what is not mine."

"She's got a bit of fever," Bessie told him. "I believe she's a bit . . . just a bit, mind, confused. The Doctor said she was to have no excitement, so we must not overwhelm her."

The tall man who stood by her bed gazed down upon her, a faint frown on his face. He was dressed fashionably and looked as if he were accustomed to doing so. How strange; there was no one in her neighborhood whose boots were so polished or who had a cravat of such elegance. There was no one who had a cravat at all. He had hair that was the color of bronze and green eyes that studied her critically. She judged him to be somewhere of age in his mid-thirties.

"The children will want to see you," he said finally after scrutinizing her for what seemed like an inordinate amount of time. "They have been concerned."

"Children? What children?"

"Our children, Gabriella," he said impatiently. "Who else? Elliot and Andrea come in to see you every day before they begin their lessons with Miss Birch. Please desist in these ridiculous games. I have no idea why you have decided to pretend that you do not know your own children but I find it despicable."

He turned and strode from the room.

Tears sprang to Gabriella's eyes. She fell back upon the pillow. "Who is he?" she whispered in a strained voice.

Bessie, uncomfortable at the scene she had just witnessed, answered, "Why, he's your husband, of course, Madame. Lord Wibberley, the Duke of Lancashire."

THE STRANGER IN THE HOUSEHOLD

*L*ord Michael strode from his wife's bedchamber, down the staircase, and into his study, his face so choleric that Simmons the butler decided that he would choose a better time to ask His Grace if he planned to dine at home tonight. Unaware that his countenance had subdued his butler, Lord Michael slammed the door of his study shut. He did not wish to be disturbed.

Of all the outrageous charades that Gabriella had ever engaged in, surely denying any knowledge of her children was the worst. Elliott and Andrea had gone in to her bedroom every day and even though she had never been a fond mother, they accorded her the affection due to her, however unreturned.

What was she about this time that she thought it worthy to feign ignorance of their existence? Would it require a new bauble for her to suddenly regain her memory?

He had been sincerely stricken when he saw her in the hospital, unconscious from a carriage accident that had required care in London's Metropolitan Hospital. When he received word of the mishap, he had rushed to the city to find his wife looking frail and broken in the bed, her eyes closed, quite unaware of what was going on around her. Paralysis of the legs, the nurse had told him in a hushed voice. A tragedy. But there was hope that she would regain the use of her legs.

However, it would be necessary to be patient, the nurse told him. That was what the doctor said. His wife had suffered an emotional as well as a physical trauma. Rest was of paramount importance and she must be kept calm. The nurse had looked weary as she spoke; there had been a fire in a nearby neighborhood that had seen deaths and injuries and the medical staff had been hurrying from patient to patient in an effort to save those who were not mortally wounded. Lord Michael was not pleased with the diagnosis or the care. But the nurse was adamant; she could not leave yet. She was not physically strong enough, the doctor had said. He could not come himself to deliver the message, the nurse said; he was trying to keep people alive.

The hospital had been a grim place and as soon as permission was granted, Lord Michael had had his wife brought to Wibberley Hall, where she could be looked after in her own home with the local doctor whose attention would be focused upon her and not on every new case that came through hospital doors.

Reliable Doctor Avery, who tended to all the finer families in Lancashire, had come as soon as Lord Michael had arrived home with Gabriella. The doctor had arranged for the hiring of two nurses to look after her. He had agreed with the London doctor's diagnosis that the Duchess must be kept calm. Paralysis, Doctor Avery explained, was a chancy matter. She would walk again, but it would not be immediate. First, she would have to regain consciousness.

Lord Michael had looked in on his wife every day. How frail she looked. It was almost possible to forget his wife's temper, her demanding nature and the delight she took in offending him, when he beheld her in her bed, dwarfed by its size. But that feeling had not lasted. She no sooner opened her eyes, Lord Michael fumed, than she was up to her old tricks again. Well, she'd be bedridden for the immediate future, and in such a condition, she would find it difficult to resume her scapegrace ways.

He decided that he would dine out tonight. There was no reason to put the staff to the trouble of preparing supper for him when he would be the only one at the table.

Below stairs, the staff learned that the Duchess had recovered, if not her mobility, at least her consciousness. Bessie had delivered the news when she went to the kitchen to relay Lady Gabriella's thanks to the cook for the broth.

Mrs. Pomeroy stared in disbelief. "Thanks? Are you sure?"

"Quite sure," Bessie said with an uncertain smile. "She was most insistent that I render her appreciation for the broth. She said it was very tasty." Bessie handed over the bowl to the cook. "She finished every spoonful. I think we should continue with broth and beef tea for several days. After that, if the Doctor agrees, perhaps we can move forward to something with a bit more substance."

Mrs. Pomeroy nodded. After Bessie left the kitchen, the cook gave the butler a meaningful glance. "Thanks?" she said.

Simmons knew that it was not appropriate to share gossip with the cook, but he and Mrs. Pomeroy had been in service together since the previous duke and they were allied in their discretion and their attention to the Wibberley family. "I suppose she may be grateful," he said dubiously.

"'Twould be the first time," Mrs. Pomeroy said. "Not a word of thanks have I ever received from Her Grace, no matter how much work I put into those dinners she hosts. Not a word of thanks when she invites guests with no notice and we have to scurry about like ants trying to get it all done in time. Scoldings, oh yes, plenty of those, if everything isn't to her liking. But never thanks."

"It's unusual," Simmons agreed. "But I have heard of invalids who discover their Christian manners after suffering an ordeal. Perhaps this is one of those incidents."

Mrs. Pomeroy was a faithful worshipper at the village church and was wont to say that she did not leave the vicar's lessons behind her when she walked out the church door. But she made no claims to being a saint, as she was also wont to say, and she had more than once voiced the opinion to Simmons that the Duchess was a nasty bit of goods. Simmons did not echo her opinion but he did not refute it.

Unaware that her simple expression of gratitude was a subject of conversation in the servants' quarters, Gabriella was intent upon her own physical condition.

"The Doctor says you may walk again," Bessie told her, "and you must be patient."

"Why am I unable to walk?"

"Because of the accident," Bessie replied patiently.

"Why do I remember nothing of any of this? I have never been in this room before and yet you and that man insist that this is my home. I do not understand any of this."

"Medical matters are often a mystery, Madam. You may ask the Doctor when he calls today."

"Today?"

"Every day, Madam. That's no more than the Duke would expect."

It was all most distressing. Gabriella felt as if her entire life until now was shrouded in some sort of blankness. There was no direct pathway to her current location. She was Gabriella Burchell, the daughter of a humble bookseller and his wife, a woman of ill health who had formerly been a nurse. She lived outside of London. She had never been to Lancashire. At least, she thought with relief, she had gotten rid of that ring and returned it to the man to whom, most likely, it belonged. It was not hers and she could not be held accountable for wearing it if she removed it from her finger. It was a very minor victory but at least she would not go to Newgate.

That, at least, would be a relief to her parents. But how would she get word to them? They would be wondering where she was; she was always a dutiful daughter who never caused them any worry. Her father was old and not in the best of health, and Mother had weak lungs.

"I must get word to them," she said, thinking out loud. She tossed the bedcoverings to one side and moved as if she would get out of bed. But her legs refused to cooperate.

Bessie, who had left her only to take her empty broth bowl downstairs and to thank Mrs. Pomeroy, on Gabriella's behalf, entered the room just in time to prevent Gabriella from toppling from the bed.

"I cannot move!" Gabriella cried out, her arms askew and her upper torso off balance from her efforts.

"Yes, Your Grace, I told you as much. Come now, put your arm around me and we'll have you to rights in no time. Now, now, there's no reason to cry. The Doctor says you'll mend. Whatever caused the paralysis isn't permanent, he says. He'll explain it all to you when he calls. You must have hope, Your Grace."

But Gabriella only cried all the more. Why was Bessie, a stranger to her, referring to her as if she had a ducal title? Either she was mad or they were.

A FAMILY FOR THE STRANGER

"**M**adame, are you well enough to see the children? They've been ever so worried about you. It would do them a world of good to see you sitting up and looking better."

The children. She leaned back against the pillows. She had slept poorly last night, her slumber interrupted by strange, intersecting dreams that collected bits of the day's events and conversations and replayed them in her mind. The realization that she was immobile, her legs paralyzed, had struck her anew with a sense of how trapped she was in this unknown identity where all those around her seemed to believe she was someone else. Worry over her parents and how they must be fretting at her absence added to the burden.

When she awoke, and pulled back the bed curtains, it was a relief to see Bessie sitting by her bed, calmly reading her

Bible. The other nurse, Louisa, had been with her from the afternoon until the nighttime; she was a pleasant-faced woman, a little older than Bessie, quiet and efficient, less inclined to conversation than Bessie. Each woman seemed competent in her task but Gabriella could not ask them to explain why they thought she was a duchess. It was all too bewildering.

The children. What should she say to them? She could hardly tell them that she was not their mother, even though she certainly was not. She would simply have to behave toward them as a mother would behave, with affection and an interest in their activities.

"Yes," she said. "After I've had a cup of tea, and perhaps some toast?"

Bessie smiled as if Gabriella had accomplished an impressive feat. "Toast, now that's what we like to hear. You're feeling strong enough to eat; The doctor will be quite glad to hear that."

The doctor had called upon her yesterday afternoon. He was a burly man who looked to be someone who spent a great deal of time out of doors; his skin was weathered by the elements and he dressed without affectation. He had told her that she must continue to rest after her ordeal, but he had not said what the ordeal was. He would be back the following day, he told her. Then he had left; she assumed that he would be delivering a report to Lord Michael but she didn't ask.

Louise and Bessie both seemed to regard the doctor as a minor deity and Gabriella saw no reason to form an opinion on his skill. She was in a place that was unknown to her, seen as the wife of a man she had never met and the mother of children she had not borne. The only absolute fact that she could not contest was that her legs were paralyzed and she did not quite have the courage to ask the doctor about that. Perhaps tomorrow . . .

"Yes . . . please ask Mrs. Pomeroy, if it's not too much trouble, if I could have marmalade on the toast?'

"Bless you, Madame, 'tis no trouble at all," Bessie said warmly. "Never you fret, if I know Mrs. Pomeroy, she'll have that piece of toast so covered in marmalade that you won't see any bread at all underneath."

"Oh, please, nothing like that. Only a very thin layer of marmalade. I don't want to use it all and leave none for somebody else."

Bessie gave Gabriella a curious gaze. "There's plenty to spare, Madame," she said at last.

"Only a thin layer, it's what I prefer," Gabriella insisted. "If you can help me wash and tend to my hair; I don't want the children to see me looking as if I'd crawled out of a grave."

She had eaten her toast and drunk her tea, and was sitting up in bed, a very pretty knitted shawl around her shoulders, when Bessie opened the door to admit two children. Elliott, the elder, was the mirror image of his father, with the same thick abundance, rather more tousled than arranged, of bronze hair and vivid green eyes. It was a shock, however, to see herself in the features of six-year old Andrea, with her curly black hair and blue eyes framed in thick dark lashes.

Gabriella, after the initial astonishment, concealed her reaction. "How have you both been?" she asked genially.

"Very well, Mama," Elliott said politely.

"You've been asleep for ever so long," Andrea pointed out.

"Yes, I suppose I have. How very lazy of me; you have both been doing your lessons and I have been quite a slug, have I not?"

Elliott laughed and then abruptly stopped, as if he had done something out of turn. Andrea's eyes widened.

"We've been very good with our lessons," she said.

"Are you listening to what your governess tells you?" What was her name? Lord Michael had used it the day before. "Are you minding her?" B, it started with a B, something to do with a tree . . . "Are you minding Miss Birch?" she inquired, triumphant at recalling the name.

"Yes, Mama," they said in unison.

"And she is not obliged to switch you too often, I trust?"

Andrea giggled. "She never does."

"Ah, so then she does not catch you when you are at your mischief. I suppose you misbehave when her back is turned," Gabriella nodded wisely. "I see how it is. I suppose that, when I am well again, I shall have to make up for all the lost punishments. To bed without supper and a spanking every morning before breakfast. Yes, I think that should take care of it."

Both children were laughing so hard that no one noticed that the bedroom door had opened.

"What is this?" Lord Michael demanded, clearly dumbfounded by the scene before him.

"Mama says she is going to spank us before breakfast," Elliott giggled.

"Fancy that," Andrea said.

Lord Michael frowned at Gabriella, who fell back against the pillows, deflated by his expression. She had only intended to be friendly to the children because, although she knew she was not their mother, they were not privy to the same information. She had attempted, however clumsily, to behave toward them as she assumed a mother would who sought to relieve her children's anxiety about her wellbeing after days and days of being unresponsive.

"Miss Birch will be wondering where you are," he said, not unkindly. He bent down and kissed each child. "Off you go now, and mind you listen."

This sent the children off into peals of laughter as they bade Gabriella farewell.

Smiling, Bessie also moved in the direction of the door. "I'll just pop down to the kitchen to see Mrs. Pomeroy about lunch," she said. It was plain that she was being tactful in assuming that Lord Michael would wish to spend time alone with his wife.

Lord Michael was dressed to go riding. "I am sure that you are eager to return to the saddle," he said.

Gabriella stared at him. "I've never been on a horse in my life," she replied. "I shouldn't know what to do."

"Gabriella, when will you stop this nonsense?" he flared. "You took to riding as soon as we were married. A day doesn't go by, unless the weather is inclement, when you do not ride. Do not think that I am cozened by those rides," he added cryptically. "I am very well aware of your antics."

"I have no idea what you are talking about, my lord," Gabriella said, caught between fury at his insistence that she was his wife and fear of his temper.

Lord Michael's gaze wandered over her features. How lovely she was, how desirable. Even though he detested her, he could not ignore her beauty. Her black hair was a tumult of curls that framed the slender oval of her face. Her blue eyes were alight with the spirit that he recalled from before the accident that had rendered her bedridden. Color flamed in her cheeks. Despite himself, his eyes were drawn to the neckline of her nightgown. She was a beauty and no woman had ever incited his desire as Gabriella had.

And no woman had ever made a fool of him as Gabriella had, he reminded himself. That beauty that he cherished had been shared with other men. She had married him for his title, wealth and position and in no time at all after their marriage, she had quickly squandered his love for her.

"I hope that you do not repeat this rubbish in front of our children," he told her angrily.

"They are not my children! I am not your wife. I do not know who you are, I do not know why I am here, and I will not be bullied by your foul temper!"

"You most certainly are my wife, and even if I shall regret marrying you until my dying day, I cannot regret the birth of our son and daughter. That, at least, is something that I have gotten from you that has not tarnished or been soiled."

"I am not your wife!"

"I shall prove that you are," he said, "and then, perhaps, you shall abandon this folly because it will not achieve whatever ends you have in mind."

He turned on his heels and stalked out of the room in a rage.

It was always the way. No one could stir him like Gabriella. Even as a convalescent, paralyzed and frail, she still had the power to move him. He was her prey.

IMAGES OF A STRANGER

"Look at it, I tell you. Look at this painting and tell me that it's not you!"

Gabriella could only weep. Lord Michael, irate at her insistence that she was a stranger to all of them, had physically picked her up in his arms and carried her to the drawing room. There, a painting of a woman who looked identical to Gabriella smiled archly at a beaming Lord Michael. The woman was dressed in what looked to Gabriella's frugal mind to be a shameful extravagance of white satin and glittering diamonds. The diamonds were arrayed around her neck, at her wrists, her earlobes, and even through her black ringlets, as if boasting of the abundance of jewels that was hers to command. Lord Michael, his gaze intent upon the woman at his side, was attired in what Gabriella recognized as the height of male fashion; polished boots, form-fitting trousers, a coat that displayed his trim, sinewy form to advantage, and a cravat so perfectly stiff that it might have been constructed of a sturdier material than fabric.

"Do you see that ring?" Lord Michael demanded. "It was my great-grandmother's ring. My great-grandfather gave it to her; he was a decorated hero of the army and he was honored by the king for his bravery. He bestowed that ring upon his wife on their wedding day and it has graced the hand of every Wibberley bride since. It is on your finger, you cannot deny it."

Still holding her in his arms as if she were weightless, Lord Michael turned around. "Look there at that painting. That is you with our children."

Again, the woman who looked exactly like Gabriella dominated the painting, seated upon a chair with her red velvet skirts falling about her. This time, she wore rubies at her throat, wrists, ears, and through her hair. At her side were younger versions of the children Elliott and Andrea. The children were scarcely noticeable, so vivid was the image of the bejeweled woman in red who smiled knowingly, and yet secretively, out of the frame.

The thought crossed Gabriella's mind that, although this woman looked like her and bore her name, she did not seem to be a particularly likeable woman. Gabriella could not explain why she sensed this, but the impression was very strong.

"I am not that woman!" she cried out.

"Your Grace," Bessie had followed Lord Michael and his captive wife out of the room and despite her sense of awe at his rank, she felt that her first duty was to her charge. "She has only recently awakened from a state of unconsciousness. She has been injured. Who is to say what she remembers or does not?"

"She is my wife!" Lord Michael thundered.

"Of course she is," Bessie said reassuringly. "But she may not—"

"I am not that woman! I am not your wife! Take me back to my room!"

"If you are not my wife, why is that your room?" he demanded.

"I don't know!" Gabriella sobbed and began to hammer at his chest with her fists.

"Take me back at once!"

"Sir, " Bessie said with a note of warning in her voice, "if the children should hear this, they would be most distressed."

"They would be distressed even more should they hear their mother deny her maternity," he returned.

"Rest is what Doctor ordered," Bessie reminded him. "This is not rest."

His jaw tightened as he considered a counter reply to her observation, but he could not refute her words. Silently, he carried his sobbing wife back to the bedroom. Despite his expression and his former words, he was gentle as he placed her back upon the bed, arranging her nightgown around her legs and pulling the bedcovers back over her.

"I did not mean to cause you discomfort," he said finally, his words emerging with reluctance as he listened to her crying. "I merely sought evidence that you are my wife and you are the mother to Elliott and Andrea. Whatever impulse of malice drives you to deny either fact must be put to rest."

Bessie said nothing until he was gone from the room. Then, as if to erase his actions, she rearranged the bedclothes around Gabriella, plumping up the pillows and then taking a handkerchief to wipe away the tears.

"There, there, Madame, it all seems dark now, to be sure, but it will brighten. The Good Book tells us so. I shall go down to ask Mrs. Pomeroy for a cup of tea and perhaps some broth. I think it must have been the beef for supper last night. Perhaps you are not ready for it yet; we must return to a milder diet for another day or so, lest you become too excitable."

"I am not being excitable!"

"No, Madame, you do not mean to be, to be sure, but I think that such food is too rich for you, in your frail state. I was overeager. We must proceed slowly. Rest, the Doctor said. Rest and no excitement. I shall tell Miss Birch that you are very tired and are not able to see the children today—"

"No! I cannot disappoint them!" Gabriella wiped her tears on the sleeve of her nightdress. It, like everything else, was a possession of that mysterious woman who looked like her and bore her name and yet was not her. The nightdress was made of soft lawn, with full sleeves cuffed with satin that fell against her skin like a fabric made of feathers. Although it was nightwear, there was something sensual in its design that made Gabriella feel as if she were a temptress. The woman who had worn this garb was a female who knew how to entice. That most certainly was not Gabriella.

Lord Michael was a brute. Perhaps they deserved each other, that siren Gabriella and the brute Lord Michael. How dare he treat her that way, swooping her up in his arms as if she were of no consequence, and carrying her as if she were a child, to force her to see paintings that, whatever they conveyed to him, merely compounded her own confusion.

"Madame, I fear that you are too distraught," Bessie said with worry plain in her tone. "An afternoon of rest is what you need."

"If I do nothing but rest, I shall certainly go mad," Gabriella replied. "I cannot lay here for hours with nothing to do but think upon my misery. At least, when the children come to visit, I am distracted for a time."

"I don't know . . ." Bessie pursed her lips. Then she brightened. "I know! We'll wait until the Doctor comes and he shall advise us."

"I shall do no such thing," Gabriella retorted, using her arms to make herself sit upright. "I am no child to wait upon the doctor's instruction. I am a grown woman of twenty-five, well able to decide for myself whether I am able to conduct a conversation with children. If I am capable of withstanding the oafish attentions of that man, I can certainly spend time with children."

Bessie sobered. It was true that Lord Michael was a man of temper, and one could not excuse the violent manner in which he had swept his Duchess up in his arms. Still, Bessie did not see Lord Michael as a man given to cruelty. That he was plainly exasperated and annoyed at his wife's inability—or unwillingness—to acknowledge her identity was obvious. But would he be so frustrated if he did not care, Bessie asked herself silently. It seemed to her that Lord Michael was a man of powerful emotions. To have his wife deny him so must be a terrible burden to bear.

Bessie was able to convince Gabriella that she would be better able to conduct herself properly with the children if she napped first. When Gabriella had finally fallen asleep, Bessie stole silently from the room, en route to speak to Mrs. Pomeroy about the tea and broth for supper. As she was on her way down the stairs, she encountered Lord Michael, on his way up.

He halted. "Miss Trask," he said.

"Sir? Your Grace?"

"I am concerned at my wife's continued state of mind. She appears to have lost her memory. When Doctor Avery comes, I wish to speak to him."

"Of course, Your Grace."

"First," Lord Michael said. "I will speak to him before he attends to my wife. I want to make sure that she is not a danger to the children."

"Oh, sir, I hardly think—"

"Can you diagnose the reason for her failed memory?"

"No, sir, but—"

"Very well, then. I shall procure an explanation from Doctor Avery. Until then, she is not to see the children."

"Sir, I don't think that is wise," Bessie disputed, emboldened. "Lady Gabriella is in no condition to do anyone any harm. Even if she had her strength, I am there when the children come. It does her much good to see them, truly it does. If she is to get better, I believe that we must do all in our power to help her."

Lord Michael permitted himself a brief, disdainful laugh. As if Gabriella cared about the children. Her jewels, her gowns, and her lovers . . . that was what his wife care for. The children? They didn't matter to her. That was why he distrusted her new-found interest in the children to be cause for alarm. Who knew what she was conspiring to do behind that feigned absence of memory? His wife was a cold and calculating Medea and he would protect his children from their mother in order to save them from harm.

MARRIED TO THE STRANGER

"You are certain?" Lord Michael refilled Doctor Avery's glass of brandy. This was not the sort of conversation which could be conducted in the presence of the servants, even the discreet Simmons, and that was why he had ordered the butler to bring the doctor to the study upon his arrival.

"I see no sign of madness, Your Grace," Doctor Avery said. "In fact, I see . . . a gentleness that is new. One could call it an early Christmas miracle.."

"Yes. That is a way one could call it..." Lord Michael said begrudgingly before downing his brandy in a single gulp. "Gentleness, you say?"

"Yes . . . . The Duchess seems to have acquired a difference in her frame of mind," Dr. Avery said, choosing his words with great care. Although his clientele was the gentry of Lancashire and he was welcome in their homes, he did not wish to imperil his standing by speaking against any of them, particularly against the Duchess herself, who was the highest-ranking female in the county. "It is not uncommon for a person in her physical condition, someone who is used to complete mobility, to be altered by the paralysis of the legs."

He held his hand over his glass to indicate that he did not want more brandy. Lord Michael shrugged and refilled his own glass. "This paralysis . . . you do not think it permanent? Is she truly paralyzed, then, or is she feigning?"

Doctor Avery was shocked. "Your Grace, there can be no disputing the condition. She cannot move her legs."

"But you say that she will regain movement," Lord Michael responded with impatience. "Why, if she will be able to walk, can she not do so now? That sounds to me as if she were not paralyzed at all."

"Your Grace, you are not a doctor," Avery told him firmly. "I can sympathize with your concern, but I assure you that the Duchess is by no means masquerading her condition. With time, she will be well again."

"And restored to her memory?"

"That is less certain," the doctor hedged. "Certainly she should recover. But we do not know what goes on in the mind. It is a hidden chamber. I do not know why she does not recall her true identity. I may only prescribe rest.

And," he added, eyeing the Duke, whose temper was visible in the tautness of his jawline and the fiery cast of his green eyes. "Tranquility."

"I am not a tranquil man, Doctor."

"If you wish your wife to make a full recovery, you surely are willing to do your part."

"I will do as much as she will," Lord Michael replied haughtily.

That was not the response the doctor had hoped for. He had heard the rumors that the Duchess, having provided her husband with an heir to the title and a daughter who would one day be married off, was not known to be keeping the marital vows of fidelity. It was his business to know what went on in the lives of his aristocratic patients so that he could prescribe, discreetly, what they needed. He knew that Lord Michael, for all that he was an arrogant man, was a conscientious master to his tenants and a respected steward of his lands. Whether the failure in the marriage was a result of his temper or the vanity of the Duchess, Avery could not say.

It would not do, Lord Michael realized, to deride the doctor as a quack for his assessment of Gabriella's status. The doctor was well regarded in the county and he was a pragmatist, as likely to prescribe brisk walks daily and a moderate diet as he was to dispense pills, for which Lord Michael was appreciative. But Dr. Avery had no idea of how cunning Gabriella could be. This pretense of a failed memory was no more than a ruse, Lord Michael was sure of that. She would probably claim that she needed to go to Bath to take the cure. Anything to get away from him.

The truth about their marriage stung. She had been the companion to an heiress and his intention, because he was five-and-twenty at the time, was to marry well, so that he could bring home a woman who would do justice to the magnificence of Wibberley and the title. But try as he would to pay court to the earl's daughter, his eye would catch sight of the black-haired, blue-eyed beauty with the ivory skin and graceful carriage, and his intentions to wed for status were for naught.

She had seemed so modest and unassuming when he finally declared himself. He had believed that she was exactly as she presented herself, a young woman of humble means, an orphan in fact, whose character was as unblemished as her countenance.

Those illusions had quickly been dashed. Gabriella, the Duchess of Lancashire, was beautiful, stylish, an excellent hostess whose wardrobe rivalled that of anyone at court. She rode like a huntress, played cards with the skill of a born gambler, flirted and danced and excelled in all the social arts of the ton. Foolish to think that such a woman would be content to give herself to only one man, and that her husband.

Lord Michael emptied the glass of brandy and put it down. He might as well go to her and discover whether she had been restored to her memory or not. He had not doubt that if he brought the Wibberley jewels to her bedside, she'd recall who she was speedily enough.

He did not knock upon her door. He opened the door and went in, and was taken aback by the sight before him. The children were sitting upon her bed, one on each side of her, and she was reading a story book to them.

"And Perseus had to be very careful not to look at Medusa, for if he did . . . " Gabriella waited expectantly.

"She would turn him to stone!" the children shouted in unison.

"Yes, and a very unpleasant thing that would be, only just think of it, to have your mighty arms wielding a sword, then, with one glance, to become a statue. Fortunately, Perseus—my lord!"

"Papa!" Andrea exclaimed. "We did not hear you come in."

"So I see."

"Mama is reading to us," Elliott explained.

"So I see. Doesn't sound very much like a Christmas story." Lord Michael glanced out the window. The first sprinklings of snow were starting to fall.

"Do you not approve?" Gabriella asked, closing the book.

"Why should I not approve? I am unused to seeing you do so, that is all. And the children have heard all of the Christmas stories already. Where is your nurse?"

"She has gone down to the kitchen to bring up a tray for us. We are going to have a picnic."

"A picnic?" Lord Michael asked, irony heavy in his tone. "Would that not be rather a challenge? Or have you suddenly discovered the use of your limbs?"

Gabriella's lower lip trembled. "No, my lord," she said in a low voice. "I have not."

He almost felt sorry for her. She seemed to be genuinely distressed. But there was nothing genuine about his wife except for her avarice, her infidelity, and her dishonesty. Those vices were genuine.

The door opened and Bessie entered, carrying a tray. "Mrs. Pomeroy has just about outdone herself, my lady," she announced. "She's sent up bread and cheese and—oh, Your Grace, beg pardon, I didn't see you."

"I seem to be quite invisible today," he observed.

"Papa, won't you join us for the picnic?"

He saw an expression of alarm display itself upon his wife's features. Of course she didn't want him there. No doubt she was planning something and enlisting the children and the nurse in her stratagem. Gabriella was more than capable of overseeing a cunning plan from her bed.

"I believe I shall," he said, watching his wife to detect a reaction.

But Gabriella maintained an impassive expression. She directed Bessie to place the tray upon the bed. She then proceeded to fill plates with the thick slices of bread that Mrs. Pomeroy had cut in the kitchen. Generous wedges of cheese followed. Bessie poured tea, generously diluted with milk for the children, into cups that the cook had provided.

"It's a splendid picnic," Andrea pronounced, biting into the bread. "And we don't have to brush the ants away."

"One generally doesn't," her father observed, "in December. More often one must brush away the snow falling atop one's head."

"Where do the ants go, Mama?" Andrea wanted to know.

"I suppose they go into the ground to sleep until the cold weather is over," Gabriella said. "And then, when people are outside again, with delicious sandwiches and cakes and lovely grapes and plums, the ants believe that it is time to return above ground, for clearly, they regard a picnic as an invitation to dine."

Oh, she was very clever, was his Gabriella, Lord Michael thought as he gravely accepted his cup of tea and his plate of bread and cheese. One would think she sincerely enjoyed the children's presence and that she enjoyed spending this time with them. One would, if one were less knowledgeable, assume that she had chosen this impromptu picnic so that she could be with them despite her supposed injury. But he was not a green boy, nor a fool, and he knew very well that she was hatching a plot. What it was, he could not guess, but she would not dupe him. And she would not malign his children against him, no matter what ploys she attempted.

WHO IS THE STRANGER?

"**W**here are the children?"

"They are with Lady Gabriella, Your Grace," Simmons replied as if it were the most ordinary thing in the world.

"They were with her this morning," Lord Michael said with a challenging air as if defying his butler to counter this fact.

"I believe they visit her every morning after their lessons, and then again in the evening before dining," the butler said.

"Do they, indeed. The Duchess, in her recuperative state, seems to be spending quite a bit of time with them."

"Yes, Your Grace. We were saying much the same thing, that it is very pleasant to see Lady Gabriella, despite her condition, taking such pleasure in the children. To be sure, she must be in considerable pain from her injuries, but never a word of complaint does she utter."

"No . . . "Lord Michael acknowledged. "I have not heard her complain either. I'm sure the servants are relieved at this new manifestation."

Simmons coughed discreetly. "It is true that she seems much more tolerant of our failings than before. The maids vie for the privilege of going into her room to tidy up."

"Do they indeed?" Lord Michael recalled a very different scenario, not so very long ago, when he had been witness to his wife's rage because none of the domestic staff seemed to be anywhere in sight when she rang for them. Everyone was very busy, apparently, too busy to attend to the capricious duchess who had been known to box their ears when they neglected to serve her morning coffee at the correct temperature. "What else do they say?"

Simmons coughed again. He was some years older than Lord Michael and his father had been the butler before him. The Simmons men were loyal to the Wibberleys. With that loyalty was born a most unusual brand of candor, between servant and master, which only manifested itself in private moments such as this, when no one else was in the room.

"They are saying, Your Grace, that perhaps Lady Gabriella died during the accident and went to heaven, and—"

"And was sent back to earth, to make restitution for her sins?" Lord Michael demanded with a bitter laugh.

"Something like that, Your Grace. She does seem to have undergone a remarkable change. A Christmas-"

"A Christmas miracle. Yes, yes. So many have said."

So Gabriella was fooling the servants as well as the children. She was a clever woman, Lord Michael thought as he climbed the staircase. Clever enough to use her physical condition, however authentic it was and Lord Michael was not entirely convinced, despite Dr. Avery's assertion that she was truly unable to move. He would catch her sometime at her masquerade and then he would expose her for the scheming vixen that she was.

He threw open the door, without knocking.

Darkness was falling early now that autumn was in season. The lamps in the room were lit, but shadows cloaked the furniture with strange outlines, making it difficult to clearly discern the boundaries between the furniture and the empty spaces.

As he drew closer, he could see that Gabriella was in her bed, and as he neared, he heard her weeping.

He halted. His wife never wept. He had never seen her shed a tear during all their years of marriage.

His features hardened. Another ruse, no doubt.

"What's amiss, Gabriella, to bring you to tears?'

She sat up. The streaks of the tears stained her cheeks. Her hair was in disarray. "Why should I not cry?" she returned. "I do not know where I am or why I am here. The servants seem to fear me even though I have never done them harm and I try not to be a bother. They hesitate at the door as if they fear that I will throw the china at them."

It was odd, Gabriella thought. Once they were inside the room, and saw for themselves that she was in good spirits, their fear seemed to fade and they were cordial, even merry, asking her what she needed and if there was anything more they could do. "No one will tell me why I am here."

Torn between familiar distrust and an unbidden pity, Lord Michael answered, "You are here because you are my wife. Where else would you be?"

"I am not your wife. I have told you so again and again," she answered wearily. "I am no one's wife. I am not married. The last thing I remember is going to bed in the home where I live with my parents. When I awoke, I was in this bed and I could not move my legs."

Lord Michael inhaled sharply. She did not sound as if she were playacting. She sounded sincere. Were her wits addled by the accident? Dr. Avery had not denied that it was impossible to know exactly what was going on inside her head. What had he said? Something about the mind being an unknown chamber. That was more so with Gabriella than with anyone Lord Michael knew and their nine years of marriage had not unraveled the mystery.

To his surprise, her tears turned into sobs as if she were exhausted by the burden of her thoughts. Of their own volition, his arms wrapped themselves around her. Too drained to resist, Gabriella leaned against him and cried.

Lord Michael said nothing. What could he say? He did not know this woman, his wife. She was a stranger. She was the woman he had married and yet she was not—

His eyes fell upon her bare shoulder, which, owing to the disheveled state of her nightgown, had fallen away from her. Her shoulder was smooth.

Where was the grotesque image that his wife, with her delight in tormenting him, had had tattooed upon her shoulder by a street artist one summer when Lord Michael had refused to indulge yet another of her extravagant wishes? That image of a yacht, a symbol of her profligacy, had irritated him beyond endurance, as she had known it would. The thought that the Duchess of Lancashire had revealed her shoulder—and who knew what else—to a common street artist was bad enough. The fact that she could, on a whim, embarrass him beyond measure if, at a ball or society event, the bodice of her gown should move and her vulgarity revealed to the assembly was even worse.

But the shoulder was devoid of anything but unmarred flesh.

Lord Michael held her tighter. He did not know who this woman was. But she was not his virago of a wife, of that, he was sure.

"It will be all right," he said tenderly. "We shall sort it all out together."

Through her sobs, Gabriella heard his soothing voice. Who was this man holding her? During the time that she had been in his manor, mistaken for his wife, he had been nothing but cold, distant and rude. Why now was he suddenly solicitous and seeking to comfort her? She was surrounded by strangers, entangled in a riddle, and no one would tell her the answer.

Gabriella pulled away from his arms, despite the fact that, for a few brief moments, it had been such a relief to draw upon his strength for comfort.

"I beg your pardon," she said. "Your shirt is wet from my tears."

She wiped her eyes with the sleeve of her nightdress, suddenly stricken with dismay when she realized that her shoulders had been exposed to the eyes of this man who thought she was someone she was not.

Lord Michael took out a fine handkerchief and began to dab at her eyes. "No pardon to beg," he said easily as the fabric moved across her face to dry her tears.

Gabriella stared at him. She did not realize that, with her long black hair tousled, her blue eyes awash with tears, her nightdress in disarray, she had a unique and unpolished beauty that, more than anything, stirred Lord Michael to feelings he could not understand himself.

Gabriella, unused to seeing him smiling, marveled at how kind he looked now. His green eyes had none of their customary arrogance; instead, they were warm and intent upon her.

"Dr. Avery says that you will regain the use of your legs," he said.

"I have felt something . . . I could not, before, feel the bedsheets against my legs, but lately, I sense them. I don't feel it as I did before, but to feel anything at all is a blessing."

"You must have your nurses assist you in trying to stand," he said. "If you can do that, perhaps it will be easier for you to attempt to walk once more. You must eat more nourishing food. Broth will not bring you to wholeness; you must have eggs and meat as well. And wine. These are foods that will sustain your strength. When I return from London, I hope to see you walking!"

Until he spoke the words, he had not realized that a plan was forming inside his head. He could not solve the mystery of this stranger until he returned to the hospital in London where his wife had been brought after her accident. Only there could he possibly learn the truth about this stranger, so like his wife and yet so completely unlike her.

"Walking by Christmas..." Gabriella said, almost to herself.

DISCOVERING TWO STRANGERS

Lord Michael ordered an early breakfast for the following morning. He intended to be on the road by sun-up and he did not plan to stop any more than he had to. Mrs. Pomeroy sent up a hearty breakfast. Lord Michael was so energized by his task that he could barely take the time to eat but he knew that he would be better served if he were not hungry. As it was, he would have to stop at inns along the way for the night before he reached London. He only had a week until Christmas day, and he always shared that with his children, though his wife had never joined them. Getting back before then was a top priority.

Before leaving, he went into the nursery to see the children, even though they were still abed. He could not delay by bidding them farewell but he knew that they would be well cared for in his absence. The servants were fond of them, Miss Birch was a kind governess and

Gabriella had proven to be more maternal than the woman who had given birth to them.

He would have stopped to see Gabriella, but he knew that her nurse would be at her bedside and he did not wish to offer explanations. Nor did he wish to awaken Gabriella if she still slept. Poor girl, she needed her rest. Whatever happenstance had brought her to Lancashire was something he needed to discover. What must it be like for her to be tangled up in this incomprehensible web?

He left Simmons with orders to explain to Lady Gabriella that business had called him away to London and that he would return home as soon as that business was resolved.

"In the meantime," Lord Michael said, "tell her that I expect her to devote her attentions to getting well. Mrs. Pomeroy is to prepare meals which will fortify Her Grace and make her strong. I hope to see her walking when I return."

"Very good sir," Simmons replied as if this were entirely expected. "Mrs. Pomeroy will do her best. She has prepared a basket for you; I've had Colm put it in the carriage. You do not travel with Lennings?"

Lennings was his valet. "No. I shall not be entertaining or being entertained on this trip to London," he told Simmons.

"Very good, sir."

"It will give Lennings time to pay court to that widow in the village that he seems to have such a fascination for," Lord Michael said with an amused grin.

Simmons raised an eyebrow. "Indeed," he murmured, wondering how on earth His Grace knew about the widow and his valet's covert visits to her cottage. "I believe, Your Grace, that the lady is quite respectable. Her husband was killed in the war."

"Yes," Lord Michael said, "I know. No doubt the banns will be announced by the time of my return."

Simmons did not know what to say to this. Lord Michael was not one to listen to tittle-tattle and Lennings was a circumspect young man. Whatever the reason, it was good to see His Grace restored to a semblance of his former good humor. The bitter marriage had eroded the jaunty young man who had ascended to his title as a child and had been known for his good humor until he had brought Lady Gabriella home.

The journey to London was a long one, affording Lord Michael the opportunity to ponder his situation. That there was a mystery in place, he had no doubt. That Gabriella, who looked exactly like his wife, minus the tattoo, and answered to his wife's name, was not his wife was plain. A tattoo could not be washed away. Therefore, this enigma was not his wife. But she must have some connection to his wife. The staff at the hospital would likely remember details of those days that he had not sought to explore when he had arrived there to bring his wife home.

He recalled that day when he received word that the Duchess of Lancashire had been in an accident. Gabriella had been in London. . . it would not be a falsehood to acknowledge that she was attending to affairs in the city while he tended to business in Manchester. They lived separate lives.

It was not pleasant to let his mind linger upon the raw pain of his marriage, which was nothing but an illusion. Society saw the Wibberleys as an attractive, stylish couple; that there was infidelity in the marriage was not unusual for members of the ton and Lady Gabriella had, after all, provided her husband with an heir who was clearly his true son. Had she been faithful until then, or had she waited until after Andrea's birth to seek her pleasures in a bed other than the one she had shared with her husband.

Their bedrooms had been separate for years. He had not found welcome in her chamber and he was too proud to beg her for intimacy. He knew that the rest of society saw him as haughty and cold. Only with his children was he able to relinquish the hauteur which shielded him from despair. He had instead derided himself for believing in the illusion of love when it was very much apparent that Gabriella had inveigled him in her own scheme so that she could escape her position as companion to an heiress, always a spectator to the excitement of the life she sought for herself but could not have. Until Lord Michael fell for her charms.

But that did not explain the puzzle of the other Gabriella, the one who wept for her sadness but did not complain of her suffering. The Gabriella who amused the children and paid attention to them, as their own mother did not do. The Gabriella who was kind to the servants instead of peremptory. It was not possible that there could be two women, identical in name and appearance, who were such opposites. And how in the world had their paths crossed at such an unpredictable moment in time?

When nightfall came, he directed his coachman to stop at the nearest inn. He intended to make very good time for the rest of the journey so that he would reach London without delay. He would be away from Lancashire for the best part of a month owing to the travel time, and there was no way to determine how quickly he would be able to accomplish his mission. In the meantime, Gabriella would be able to mend and work toward her own recovery. Mrs. Pomeroy would see to it that Gabriella ate well, of that there was no doubt. The cook was fond of Gabriella—this Gabriella, he corrected himself—and where her loyalty was engaged, so was her culinary zeal.

Lord Michael was correct in his assessment. The nurses and the household staff were united in their efforts to help Gabriella regain her mobility as soon as they learned from Bessie that she was experiencing sensation in her legs. Louisa, the night nurse, avowed that massages would help the muscles strengthen and with that aim in mind, she tirelessly followed through on her prediction. Gabriella was surprised that the massages did seem to be helping; she could feel a tingling in her legs after Louise's rigorous ministrations were concluded. Or perhaps, she thought with a quirk of amusement, it was the hot wine that Mrs. Pomeroy prepared for her before she went to bed, so that she would sleep easily despite the treatment her nurse provided. Mrs. Pomeroy believed in cures that could be eaten and drunk more than she had faith in massages or medicines.

The cook had begun coming to Gabriella's bedroom in mid-morning to go over the meals for the day. As she told Simmons with some satisfaction, it was a pleasure to work with Her Grace, so willing she was to listen to Mrs. Pomeroy's suggestions.

"And none of this hoity-toity food that no one can pronounce," she declared when she returned to the kitchen with the day's meals planned. "She's very content with good English beef and mutton, cooked as I've always cooked them."

"She does seem to be much more amenable to listening," Simmons agreed.

"I warrant His Grace will be in a better temper when he returns," Mrs. Pomeroy said. "P'haps it isn't such a bad thing, her not being able to walk."

"Mrs. Pomeroy!"

"I only meant that those as can't walk aren't likely to be going where they oughtn't," Mrs. Pomeroy answered cryptically.

"I doubt that His Grace would prefer his wife to remain an invalid for the rest of her life."

Mrs. Pomeroy said nothing. The ways of the aristocrats were beyond her ken. But it was true that illness had gentled the imperious Duchess. Who could blame the Duke if he preferred an invalid wife and a tranquil home life to an adulteress who preferred London society to her own family?

WHO IS THE STRANGER?

"*D*octor Hennessey? I am—"

"I remember you," replied the doctor, a lean man, stoop-shouldered, who looked as if he needed to eat heartier meals and sleep longer hours. He had a kindly face with tired eyes and a gentle smile. "How is your wife, Your Grace?"

"You remember her?" Perhaps this would not be such a Herculean task after all, Lord Michael thought with hope. If the doctor remembered the circumstances of his wife's time in the hospital, surely he could reveal more about what happened and how he had ended up taking home a woman who was not his wife, but was enough like her in looks to be her twin.

"She is improving," Lord Michael answered cautiously. *But she is not my wife.*

That was not something he was prepared to share with the good doctor, however, or with anyone. "She has not yet regained the use of her legs, I fear. But what concerns me is her memory. She has no recollection of who she is. She insists that she does not know me, that the children are not our children, and that she lives in London, not Lancashire."

"Please sit down," the doctor directed. His office was rather cluttered with medical paraphernalia. He cleared a stack of what looked to be rather dreary medical books off a chair and gestured for Lord Michael to sit down. Slightly amused, Lord Michael did so. Clearly, in a medical environment, there was no deference shown for a title; the doctor was the only aristocrat who mattered.

"Will you take tea, Lord Michael?"

Lord Michael declined. "I am sure that you are a busy man and I have no wish to take up too much of your time."

"It is actually one of the quieter days we've had. Everyone's at home preparing for Christmas and a lot less prone to accidents." Dr. Hennessey said with his mild smile. "Nothing like the day when your wife arrived."

Lord Michael leaned closer to the desk. "Perhaps tea would be beneficial after all," he said. "If you are certain that it would not be an imposition."

The doctor rose from his chair and went to the door, where he instructed someone out of view to bring tea.

"Not at all," he assured Lord Michael, sitting back down. "My staff delights in coddling me. They are excellent workers. I am very fortunate."

Considering that the doctor's collar was frayed and his coat looked as if it had seen better days, Lord Michael could have disputed the adjective, but he could see that the doctor was a kind-hearted man.

"You mentioned the day that my wife was brought in," he prodded gently to return the doctor to the subject foremost on his mind. "You recall it?"

"It would be impossible to forget, although I must confess that, in the frenzy of that day, I do not remember specific details. Why do you ask? It is not uncommon for persons suffering from an injury to the spine to suffer punishment to their limbs. A young woman was brought in that day with a spinal injury. There was an outbreak of fire in the row of houses in her neighborhood. She was fortunate; a beam fell upon her and hurt her waist, but she did not perish in the flames. The same, alas, was not true of her parents, who died. There were a great many patients to see to that day. Most of them, unfortunately, could not be helped."

"My wife was not injured in a fire," Lord Michael said, a trifle impatiently. "There was an accident with a carriage. She was hurt."

Dr. Henessey rubbed his eyes. "Yes . . . " he said slowly. "I think I recall. I saw her briefly, but Dr. Mason attended to her. Most tragic, of course; the young man with her was killed."

Young man? What young man? Lord Michael held himself in check. Best not to say too much or Dr. Hennessey, out of discretion, would censor himself. "Yes, I believe he was," Lord Michael said. "Tragic."

"Dr. Mason will likely tell you the same things that I have regarding spinal injuries, but if you would feel better talking to him, I would be happy to take you to him---ah, thank you nurse, tea will be most welcome. It's a very raw day out there."

"Here you go then, Doctor," the nurse said as she carried in the tea tray. She gave Lord Michael a scrutinizing glance that seemed to indicate his lack of worthiness at being in the doctor's presence. "Just let me know if you want more. See that you eat a sandwich; you're nothing but skin and bones. You work too hard and that's the truth." With a final glance at Lord Michael, as if warning him not to tire the doctor, the nurse left the office.

Dr. Hennessey smiled. "I am very fortunate. Sugar?"

"Yes, please. I wonder . . . when my wife came in, was she aware of her surroundings?"

Dr. Hennessey shook his head as he stirred sugar into his tea. "No, she was not conscious. She was very weak and her injuries were severe. To tell you the truth, I was surprised when I learned that she had survived. I should not have thought it possible. I suspected some damage to the head which could have caused bleeding. We could do nothing about that. But as you have seen, she recovered. It is most heart-rending when we must deliver sad news to family members. The family of the young man who was injured with your wife—a relative of yours, no doubt—was most afflicted with grief when they learned of his end. He was French; his father is something in the embassy. Well, I've no need to be telling you this, as he is a relative."

"Actually," Lord Michael said carefully, "he was from my wife's side." As he offered this cursory explanation, Lord Michael realized that he had known about his wife's affair with the dashing and dissolute Comte de Bellevoir for a long time. It had not wrenched his heart, it had scalded his pride and for that reason, he had maintained an air of oblivious indifference to where she was going or whom she was seeing when he was with her in London and she was so often away from home until very late in the night. "I barely knew him, to tell the truth. French."

It was enough for an Englishman to offer as an explanation. The doctor nodded. "We had a devil of a time trying to identify everyone; between the fire and the accident, it was rather chaotic at the hospital. We never have so many patients all at one time as we did that day. As you may imagine, two terrible disasters within hours of each other strained our resources considerably. Dr. Mason and I are generally adequate for the medical needs of the community, but on that dreadful day, we barely had time to consult one another on patients. We do not customarily share patients, you understand, but there was no time, between those suffering from burns and those from injuries. It was not how we like to practice medicine. I pray that we offered all the care that we could." The doctor's lined face brightened. "But you tell me that your wife is recovering, and that does gladden my heart. That such severe injuries were not fatal is, you understand, nothing less than a divine miracle."

How refreshing to hear a different word in front of miracle. "Yes . . . was my wife one of the patients whose care was divided between you and the other doctor?"

"Yes. I saw to her when she was brought in, but I did not do anything further. I did not expect her to survive, you see," Dr. Hennessey said apologetically. "There were others who had a chance. I had to make the choice. Dr. Mason took over at some point; it was during the night . . . we did the best we could."

"Yes, I can perceive the circumstances under which you and your associate were laboring. It could not have been easy. I wonder, would I be imposing if I also spoke to Dr. Mason? I suppose I met him when I came to take my wife home to Lancashire, but I was not in a very coherent state at that point. I only remember that a nurse told me that the doctor's orders were that my wife was not yet well enough to leave. Even when it was determined that she could travel, she was not yet conscious."

"Yes . . . spinal injuries require special attention. I am sure that Dr. Mason will be glad to speak with you . . . that is . . . I hope you will not be offended. My associate is of a somewhat curt nature and that is sometimes taken as rudeness. He does not mean to be rude."

Lord Michael smiled. "You need not worry. I myself am often regarded as abrasive in my manner. I expect that Dr. Mason and I will understand one another well enough.

THE MYSTERY OF THE STRANGERS DEEPENS

Gabriella was mystified by Lord Michael's sudden departure and equally puzzled by his instructions to her and to the staff that she was to be fed particularly nourishing food to hasten her improvement.

Perhaps he wanted her to be well enough so that he could turn her out, she thought as she surveyed the tray in front of her. She wasn't his wife and therefore she had no claim upon his charity. She only wished that someone would allow her to send a message to her parents, but she was unsure of how to request this. Perhaps, with Lord Michael away for an extended amount of time, she would be able to come up with a solution. The household regarded her as the Duchess of Lancashire; in his absence, they would be likely to heed her instructions. She needed to know about her parents' wellbeing and to reassure them that she was well.

She had managed to regain enough movement in her legs so that she could, with Bessie's help, accomplish the few steps from the bed to the table by the window so that she could eat. She had protested at continuing to take her meals in bed and Dr. Avery had consented to let her leave her bed for brief periods of time, as long as she had the stamina to do so.

Mrs. Pomeroy, enlisted to prepare meals that whetted Gabriella's appetite while furthering the instructions to develop menus which aided her recovery, had spared neither effort nor expense.

The lunch tray that was presented to her included a chicken breast cooked in wine and stuffed with chestnuts. Pickled vegetables that had been put up from the Wibberley gardens made a bright splash of color upon the delicate china. There was a thick slice of bread covered in freshly churned butter; generous wedges of cheese from the Manor's dairy; and for dessert, pie made from the apples that came from the estate's orchard. A glass of wine, liberally poured, finished off the meal.

"It's rather . . . a lot," Gabriella said.

"The Duke is eager to see you well, my lady," Bessie assured her. "Mrs. Pomeroy will be so disappointed if you do not like it."

"I like it well enough, but three people could dine on this and leave the table loosening their buttons. Bessie, I must begin to dress again, but I have no clothes. I cannot continue to spend the days in night clothing."

"But Madame, your closets are full of clothes," Bessie protested. "After you eat, I'll bring in several frocks for you to choose from."

"I'd dearly love a bath," Gabriella said longingly. "Just a basin to wash from every morning isn't enough."

"I don't know . . . I'm not sure that you're steady enough on your feet to manage getting into a tub. We'll check with Dr. Avery," she decided.

"If eating three full meals a day is not enough to restore my health, I fail to see what Dr. Avery can do about it," Bessie said with asperity. "I intend to have a bath this afternoon. And I'm going to wash my hair. And I want to read newspapers; I know nothing of what is going on in England. If I continue to behave like an invalid, I shall become one."

When Bessie brought Gabriella's requirements to Dr. Avery's notice upon his call, he was quick to agree. "When a patient is that eager to leave the sickbed, nurse, we must support them."

"She's still a bit wobbly, though, sir," Bessie said uncertainly. "I shouldn't like her to take chances."

"Taking chances is part of getting better. Please convey my remarks to her. As she is taking her bath, I shall not intrude. I daresay she's welcoming the experience and will likely linger."

"Indeed she is, sir. I've poured more hot water in twice. I did make her promise not to try to get out until I'm there to help her."

"Very good. You are committing yourself admirably, nurse. My compliments. There is going to be a considerable amount of work for you in the village when you are no longer needed here. I think that we may safely predict that such an event will occur and the Duchess will be able to resume her usual routine at some point."

Dr. Avery wondered if the new routine would include a resumption of the Duchess' previously licentious ways. But he was not a clergyman; the souls of his patients were not for him to heal.

Lord Michael, upon being introduced to Dr. Mason, reflected that the medical calling attracted men of very different temperaments. He had been familiar with Dr. Avery for all of his life and appreciated the doctor's practical ways and manner. Dr. Hennessey was deferential and serene, committed to his work with a temperament that accommodated the demands of his profession. Dr. Mason was a short, stocky man who conveyed a sense of energy with every movement, as if he were stirring up the cosmic forces at each step. His bow upon introductions was brief and perfunctory, a concession to courtesy but not a surrender to rank.

"How may I help you, Your Grace?" he asked in a tone which indicated that he had better things to do and little enough time to do them.

Lord Michael smiled. "May I sit down?"

"If you must," Dr. Mason conceded grudgingly. He sat upon the edge of the chair behind his desk as if, at any moment, an emergency would summon him from the room.

"I have some questions, as I am sure you can appreciate, regarding my wife's condition when she was here."

"I was told she is recovering," Dr. Mason said brusquely. "What questions have brought you all the way to London? Surely you must have had to travel through snowfall, and mere days before Christmas too. You have a physician in your village who could have answered them don't you?"

"Our village doctor is most capable, but he did not attend to her care when she was first injured," Lord Michael said, keeping his impatience on a leash.

Dr. Mason waved an imperious hand. "Doctors do much the same thing; it is contingent upon the injury."

"My wife came home unconscious. When she awoke, she had no memory of what had transpired. She insists that she is not my wife."

"Memory loss is, unfortunately, a common symptom of injuries of this nature."

"Do you recall my wife?"

Dr. Mason stared at Lord Michael, who stared back.

"Your Grace," Dr. Mason began as if awarding Lord Michael his title was a concession he would have preferred not to make, "do you have any notion of the number of patients we treated during those hours? There was Dr. Hennessey and myself, and our nurses and orderlies. We worked without sleep that night and the day after as well, struggling to keep as many patients alive as we possibly could. You can have no idea what an effort was made on behalf of your wife and the patients who were in much worse shape."

"Much worse shape? According to Dr. Hennessey, my wife is lucky to be alive! He said that she endured such physical trauma from the accident that he did not expect her to survive."

"Dr. Hennessey is confusing your wife with other patients. Your wife was in no danger of dying. She endured an injury from a falling beam in the fire; it was certainly not pleasant and it afflicted her with paralysis, but she was not at death's door. The night was tragic enough; it does not need your melodrama to make it worse."

"My wife – what are you saying?"

"I am saying that your wife was injured in the fire. She did not suffer burns, for which you should be eternally grateful. But a beam from the burning house—one of the burning houses, I should say, as the fire raged through a row of them, all along the street, with great loss of life and property—struck her waist. She was brought to the hospital. Eventually, I saw her and the nurse tended to her injuries and kept her comfortable so that the pain would not be unbearable. She remained alive, as I expected she would do. Word was sent to you. By the time you arrived, Lancashire being some distance from London, her physical health had improved, although she remained unconscious."

"My wife's name is Gabriella," Lord Michael said slowly. "She has black hair and blue eyes."

"I do not recall what color her eyes were as she did not open them. We pried open her lids to examine her, of course, but you will pardon me, I trust," Dr. Mason said sarcastically, "if I failed to find the sight so memorable that I can recall the color of her eyes. Yes, the woman had black hair and yes, her name was Gabriella. I remember it. Now, if you have had enough of your questions answered, I am a busy doctor and my patients await."

WHO IS THE STRANGER?

"Old newspapers will do very well," Gabriella said. "I have been so long isolated that I must catch up on past events." Now that she was beginning to feel better, she wanted her mind as well as her body to improve. Her father had been devoted to daily newspapers so that he could follow the events of the day and he had enjoyed discussing the stories with Gabriella. She had requested Bessie to bring her newspapers so that she could continue that practice, even without her father at her side. It was much easier to make these requests with Lord Michael gone; she realized, with no small amount of surprise, that in his absence, she was regarded as the authority of the household and her wishes were sought on all matters from the approval of the household accounts to the final plans for Christmas.

"I rescued these from the maid; she was about to pitch the lot into the fire."

"Thank you. Will you invite the children to join me for lunch after they have finished their lessons with Miss Birch? I can only do justice to Mrs. Pomeroy's excellent cooking if I have their assistance."

Bessie beamed. "They'll be delighted, I've no doubt."

Gabriella smiled. "I hope they are hungry. Thank you, Bessie."

"You won't be getting up, will you?" Bessie asked anxiously.

Gabriella patted the comfortable settee upon which she reclined. "I shall idle here, reading old newspapers and sipping tea and feeling as if I am quite the lady of leisure," she said.

Bessie's smile faded. "So you are, Madame," she said. "You are a duchess. You still don't remember?"

Gabriella sighed. "No," she answered. "Nothing. I don't know where I am from, but it is assuredly not Lancashire. I am from London."

"You speak like a toff," Bessie said. "You sound like a duchess, truly you do."

"Having known none, I cannot say how I sound when I speak. But my parents are not aristocrats. My mother is a nurse, my father owns a bookstore. They are not without education, but they make no pretensions to being more than humble folk."

"Perhaps it will come to you," Bessie said hopefully.

"Yes, but in the meantime, my parents must be fretting dreadfully about where I am. We are very close; it's only the three of us and as you may imagine, as we see each other daily..."

Bessie pulled a handkerchief from her apron pocket and quickly applied it to the tears that had begun to fall from Gabriella's eyes. Dr. Avery had been firm in his injunction that they must not humor the Duchess in her delusions that she was someone else. How could she ever recognize her true identity, he had explained to the nurses, if she was humored in her belief that she was a Londoner of humble beginnings? It made sense and Bessie tried to heed his advice; he was the doctor, after all, and she but a humble nurse. Still, when Madame was reduced to tears over thinking that her poor parents were wondering where she was, it was not easy to regard the matter Doctor's logic.

She had an idea that would ease Madame's worry while not circumventing Doctor's orders. "Maybe there's a way, Madame . . . do you remember your London address?"

"Of course I do," Gabriella responded. "Why?"

"What if we post a letter to your parents, telling them that you are well and recovering from your injuries?"

"They shall wonder what injuries I am referring to."

"We'll come up with something that won't make them fret, but will reassure them that you are well. Plenty of people go to the country to get better."

"Not at the onset of winter, they do not," Gabriella said drily. "But your plan has merit. I shall compose a letter this afternoon and if you can have it posted, I shall be able to ease my parents' fears that I have vanished."

"Right you are, Madame," Bessie smiled. "You write your letter and I'll post it myself."

Still in London, Lord Michael was on a similar errand in his efforts to unravel the mystery of the two Gabriellas. It was obvious that two women, identical in appearance but strangers to one another, had been brought to the hospital at the same time: one, the Duchess of Lancashire, had been seriously wounded in a carriage accident involving other people in which her lover—for there was no denying at this stage the identity of the young man who was with her—had been killed; and a fire which had swept through a row of houses, burning many of the inhabitants and causing injury to others, including the woman who looked so much like his wife and yet could not be. The tattoo proved that. But he needed evidence. What he would do with that evidence, Lord Michael did not know. The woman he had married was dead. The woman at Wibberley Hall was not his wife. But that alone did not explain their resemblance or their names.

Despite Dr. Mason's disinclination to provide further help, Lord Michael was able to exert a bit of charm on one of the nurses who had been at the hospital that night. She told him where the neighborhood was located where the fire had taken place. It had, she told him, wiped out an entire street; nothing left but ruined buildings and rubble. "It was," she said, "ever so sad to look upon," because of the remnants of belongings that remained behind. Children's toys and household goods, here and there a shoe, or a cane, or some other item that bespoke of better times. Lord Michael gave her a sovereign for her help; she was reluctant to accept it, but did so after he assured her that she had been of inestimable assistance in his search, and that she should take it as a Christmas present. He did not specify what he was searching for and the nurse, furtively pocketing the coin, did not ask. It was a great deal of money for a bit of information, she thought as she returned to her work, but likely he could afford it.

Energized by the information, Lord Michael directed his driver to take him to the neighborhood on the outskirts of London where the fire had taken place. It was as the nurse had told him. The rubble was not yet entirely cleared away; with it being the harshest winter in years, he supposed that the work would have to wait until the spring. There was an entire block where nothing remained of any height; charred wood was strewn upon the ground, a memento of the houses that had once stood. A layer of snow, blackened by ash and charred wood, lay across the scene.

The other side of the street was occupied by houses which appeared to be well cared for. It was not a wealthy neighborhood but it indicated a community where the people, if not rich, were not mired in poverty. He hailed a housemaid who was passing by. She gave him a wary glance as if suspicious of his intentions.

He realized that giving the virtuous housemaid money for her information would not be wise; the street was busy and occupied and she would be anxious to preserve her reputation from the curious eyes of passers-by.

He got to the point of his errand quickly.

"Excuse me, miss, I wonder if I might trouble you for some information about the fire that burned these buildings back in the late summer?"

"'Twas a terrible thing," she said.

"Yes, I am sure of that. I am looking for someone who lived here. Her name was Gabriella."

"What would the likes of you be wanting with Gabby?" she asked. "The Burchells was honest folk."

Burchell. Gabriella—Gabby Burchell. This was, or had been, the street where she had lived until that fateful night when a fire had robbed her of her home.

"I am sure of it," he said promptly. "I did not know Miss Burchell prior to the fire, but circumstances have since arisen which have acquainted me with her."

"Not likely," the maid said. "She's in the church cemetery, her and her parents. They all died in the fire."

"The church cemetery? Could you direct me to it?"

"I've work to do and my mistress will not thank me for lollygagging to speak to a stranger," she declared. "If it's information about the fire that you're looking for, you might as well go and speak to Mrs. Ida Burchell. The Burchells were her kin."

"Where might I find Mrs. Burchell?"

The housemaid, anxious to be on her way, gave him directions. Lord Michael thanked her and got back into his carriage. It appeared as though he might be on his way to obtaining answers to the mystery of the two Gabriellas.

FALLING IN LOVE WITH A STRANGER

The trees were barren of leaves and the Lancashire countryside was experiencing even heavier snow than London was, by the time that its Duke returned. Instead of going straight to Wibberley Hall, Lord Michael directed his coachman to stop at Dr. Avery's home. It was nearly evening and darkness was falling, shrouding the lanes of the village in shadow. It was the Christmas Eve; his journey back had been a slow one due to all the snow. He could rush home, but he needed to confer with the doctor before he returned home. The night was still young, and he would be home before midnight.

As he had hoped, Dr. Avery was home. The housekeeper brought him to the dining room where the doctor was finishing his tea.

"Your Grace," Dr. Avery said, rising. "Will you join me?"

"Thank you, I will. It's a cold night."

"It was a cold day. I'm expecting a Christmas celebrated by the warm fire indoors, rather than the usual outdoor excursions." Dr. Avery said. "At least the harvest was a good one; people won't go hungry. It won't hold off the illnesses, but they'll be stronger and better able to fight it."

He poured tea and added a generous dash of brandy. "What brings you here? You've been gone a good while. The Duchess is doing very well. She's walking. Not very far or fast," he added at Lord Michael's pleased expression. "But she is making great strides. She takes her meals sitting at the table in her bedchamber and she insists on dressing for the day instead of remaining in bed. I have no doubt that her exertions bring her some pain, but she has not complained nor has she asked for anything to bring her comfort. She is doing well."

"I am glad to hear it."

"And your search?" Dr. Avery knew of Lord Michael's mission to London and its purpose. The two had been in correspondence during the weeks that Lord Michael had been gone so that Lord Michael could be kept abreast of Gabriella's progress and also provide Dr. Avery with any relevant medical details that he was able to learn.

"Revelatory but it is not likely to be pleasant for Gabriella."

Lord Michael explained what he had learned from Ida Burchell, Gabriella's aunt. "She took me to the cemetery. The Burchells are buried there; there is a gravestone marking the burial site for Gabriella Burchell. Avery, the birthdate is the same as my wife's."

"Why is the Duchess of Lancashire buried in a church graveyard in a neighborhood outside London?"

"I don't know. I must tell Gabby—that is what her family called her—what I have learned, but I am concerned. How will she take the news that her parents are dead? And that there is a grave with her name on the marker?"

"I advise against it," Dr. Avery said immediately. "She is progressing well. Such news could deliver a setback which could do her actual physical and emotional harm. Despite her advances, she remains in a fragile state."

"But surely it is not fair to her to let her continue to doubt her own sanity. She has insisted all along that she is not the Duchess of Lancashire and that this is not her home."

"She is not ready for such news," Dr. Avery insisted. "As her doctor, I strongly recommend that you refrain from telling her until she is stronger. And what of you?" he asked, his keen perceptions alerting him that the Duke was struggling with the information that he had unearthed.

"I . . . do not know," Lord Michael answered evasively. The truth was that he had learned much more from Ida

Burchell than where her relatives were buried. But how could he tell Gabby the truth? "I suppose I shall wait until I see for myself what progress she has made."

"It seems to me," Dr. Avery said, "that you are by way of falling in love with this woman."

"I was in love with Gabriella when I married her."

"And she, it seems, is gone. Yet you have a wife who looks exactly like her and bears her name and, you say, was born on the same date. It is most unusual, to say the least."

"Most unusual." Lord Michael drank the last of his tea and rose. "I must return. I have been away a long time. And I must be home for Christmas, or my children will sorely miss me. As I'm sure they are missing me right now."

"The Duchess has been a very good mother," Dr. Avery told him. "I daresay they miss you, but not as much as they would have had she not been there. It is a remarkable situation."

Lord Michael did not ask the doctor what he meant. He already knew.

Lord Michael's plan to return home that night was thwarted, however, as the snow had kept falling. It had fallen so thick that his carriage wheels would spin freely, or worse, get trapped in the snow. When he made an attempt to stride the rest of the way home, Dr. Avery quickly put a stop to that, saying the children didn't need two dead parents. His bluntness quickly snapped Lord

Michael out of stubbornness, and he painfully and somberly resigned to sleep in one of the good doctor's spare rooms.

When he eventually was able to arrive home the night morning – Christmas morning - Simmons took his cloak and hat and updated him as the lord rushed in. The children were well, the Duchess was well. During his absence, they had not used the dining room, as the Duchess was unable to descend the stairs. The children, who had never dined formally with their parents anyway, had taken their lunch and supper with the Duchess. It being Christmas, they are also to share breakfast with the Duchess.

"Then I suppose I must ask Mrs. Pomeroy to set another place for me in my wife's bedroom so that I, too, may join them," Lord Michael said. "Please tell Linnings that I will change for breakfast. Is he at home?"

Regrettably, he was not. "Not knowing that you would be arriving this night," Simmons said.

"Then I shall have to see to my own attire," Lord Michael said. "I assume that he will be coming back tonight?"

"Your Grace!" Simmons said is disapproval. "The widow is a most virtuous lady."

"No doubt she is," Lord Michael grinned as he began to climb the staircase. "But Lennings is unlikely to be as virtuous. I think they ought to marry as soon as possible before this paragon's reputation is in ruins."

Simmons smiled. "I am sure that Lennings will appreciate your blessing."

"Oh and Simmons," Lord Michael paused and smiled. "Happy Christmas."

Simmons' smile got even wider. "Merry Christmas, sir."

It was good to be home, Lord Michael reflected as he changed his traveling clothes as quickly as he could. He had never been fond of London. Perhaps that was because his wife had preferred it. What would Gabby think? How was he to pursue his courtship of the woman? For, during his time away, Lord Michael had come to the realization that he was in love with the stranger who, against all expectation, had been brought to Wibberley Hall as his wife weeks ago.

He had not been very charitable toward her, he realized. He had apologies to tender and wooing to do, and explanations . . . it was all very jumbled. How could he court a woman who was already seen as his wife, and how would she react to learning from him that her parents were dead and her home destroyed, and that she was believed to be dead as well?

He had not revealed to Ida Burchell, a respectable widow of a clergyman, the reasons for his questions, offering only an alibi that he had known people who were killed in the fire and he sought to place a memorial in the local church. Mrs. Burchell had been very grateful. It had taken some coaxing, but she had opened up about the family and it was then that Lord Michael had been regaled with the shocking story of the Gabriellas. He had the answers that he sought in his quest to discover how two women with the same name and appearance could have lived such disparate lives. But those answers would be unsettling for Gabby.

He knocked on the door of her bedroom then went in without waiting for a response. He saw her seated at the table. In her hands was a newspaper.

She was sobbing.

"My dearest," he said, hurrying to her side. This time, she was attired in one of Gabriella's dresses; he recognized it. Her hair was simply arranged in a chignon at the base of her neck instead of loose upon her shoulders.

She turned to him, not resisting when he gathered her into his arms. "Whatever is the matter?" he asked with concern.

She showed him the newspaper. "My parents are dead!" she burst out. "There was a fire. That is how I came to my injury. But they died in the fire. The entire street was destroyed by flames. My parents are dead!"

He held her as she cried. "I know," he said finally. "I went to London to find out what happened. It was then that I discovered the truth. I saw your parents' graves. I'm so very sorry, my dearest."

"Why are you calling me that?"

"Because..." he could not continue. It would be too much for her to absorb.

"Because you are sitting up and Dr. Avery tells me that you are doing very well."

"It doesn't matter," she exclaimed. "My parents are dead and my home is gone. What shall I do?"

"There is nothing that you can do now," he said gently. "Your parents are gone, but you are not alone."

"No, I have family, but Aunt Ida cannot take me in, she has only a pittance from Uncle Frederick's inheritance. He was a clergyman and had very little to leave her when he died."

"I know."

"How could you know?" she demanded.

"I have been to London. I have spoken to your Aunt Ida. I saw the graves of your parents. We shall discuss this later. I wish to dine with my family on Christmas morning, and as you are not able to manage the stairs yet, we shall dine en famille here." Taking his handkerchief, he dried her tears. "Let's not distress the children. I am very grateful to you for taking such excellent care of them in my absence.

Dr. Avery has been singing your praises. Where is your nurse?"

"I no longer need anyone at my bedside constantly," she told him. "Bessie and Louisa take turns during the day. They have been very helpful but I do not wish to be treated like an invalid and I want to do as much as I can. They also have families to share Christmas morning with, so I freed them to do so. You said that you spoke to Aunt Ida?"

"Yes; she is an estimable woman and I shall speak more of this after we have eaten. I know that it is asking a great deal of you, but I beg you to wait until the children have opened their presents and are satisfied to go and play. Then we will discuss the entire matter. I promise you that I shall listen to you."

Gabriella bravely rubbed another tear out of her eye. "Of course. I hope they like the presents I have picked out for them."

Lord Michael's eyebrows raised in surprise. "You chose presents for them yourself?"

Gabriella nodded. "And for you too. I am very sorry, the servants must have used your money to purchase them, as I gave none of my own. Since I have my own."

A warm smile broke out on Lord Michael's face. This certainly was a very different Christmas.

BELOVED STRANGER

When the children came into the room, they noticed immediately that Gabriella had been crying. Lord Michael told them that it was because she was so happy to see that he had returned. Gabriella did not dispute this; her brain was in a fever at the news that her beloved parents were gone. Her life in London, the life that she knew, was destroyed and what was left was this façade in Lancashire, where she was believed to be a duchess and the wife of the man sitting across from her at the dainty table where, presumably, his real wife had opened her mail and conducted her duties as the lady of the household.

Lord Michael, aware of Gabriella's preoccupation and sympathizing with it, kept the children diverted, lifting both of them up in warm embraces, wishing them both the happiest of Christmas. After they had all eaten breakfast, Michael had presents brought out for the two of them which they opened with excitement. The presents Gabriella had gotten them filled them with even more excitement, as they had been informed by the many times the children had spoken with her at lunch and dinner. The personal touch of the presents from a woman who had seemingly never cared before almost brought Andrea to tears.

After all the excitement, Lord Michael told Gabriella that he would return after he brought the children up to the nursery.

Gabriella, who had barely touched her meal, though had smiled warmly at the gifts giving, did not know whether to dread his return or to anticipate it.

That he had gone to London to discover for himself the reasons why she had told him she was not his wife was both reassuring and troubling. Her parents were dead and she had not even been there at the funeral. What must Aunt Ida think of her? How would anyone ever understand? She had loved her parents and would have been there to grieve with the other mourners. But why had she not been there? She hoped that Lord Michael would be able to provide answers to this unbearable mystery.

"Come in," she called when she heard the knock on the door. He had not been used to knocking; that he did so now instead of abruptly entering was another indication that circumstances had changed, but she could not conceive of how. He knew that she was not his duchess; why then, should his manner change to one of solicitude?

"The children loved the presents," he said as he came to the table. "They have never received such thoughtful gifts from their mother before." A moment of awkward silence sat in the air. They both knew Gabriella wasn't their mother. "I understand from Simmons that it has become customary for them to dine with you."

"I apologize if I have introduced a habit which is unsuitable to your status. As you know, I am not a duchess and in my family, we dined together from the time I was old enough to manage my fork. I had no nanny or governess; Aunt Ida took care of me. My mother was a nurse but declining health forced her to leave a profession that she loved. My father managed a bookshop in the city. They were simple people, with no grandeur to elevate them to any status that would impress anyone. I have never pretended otherwise."

"I am not accusing you," Lord Michael said quietly. "I must beg your pardon for my behavior toward you. Will you let me explain why I acted as I did?"

"It is of no significant. I must make my way in the world on my own. I shall not trouble you any longer than I must. As soon as I am well, I shall return to London. Perhaps Aunt Ida will let me live with her. I shall find work and we shall manage, the two of us. I am grateful to you for the expense and effort that you have provided for my recovery."

"Gabby," he said, "please let me speak. I certainly wish for you to recover. But . . ." he paused. This was difficult; he was a proud man. "I hope that you will stay here with me and the children. You have become part of their lives and when I explain the circumstances of my marriage, I think you will understand why I now feel as I do."

Haltingly, he told her the truth of his marriage. The beautiful Duchess of Lancashire was venal, not noble. He had been trapped in a marriage so unhappy that he had avoided his wife whenever possible. As she had preferred to live in London and away from him, the parting had not been difficult. But even when he was obliged to be in London for business, their marriage had been an illusion.

"She was leaving me to run away with her lover, a French count of dissolute habits. On the way, there was a carriage accident; a number of people were killed. My wife was taken to the nearest hospital. The doctor who first saw her doubted that she would survive, so severe were her wounds. Later that night, there was a terrible fire that spread to all of the houses on one street; residents were brought to the hospital, many of them suffering from burns which would take their lives. The doctors did what they could for the patients. There were also patients who were not burned, but who suffered injuries from falling beams. You were one of those patients; a beam toppled and hit your waist. You were brought to the hospital and the doctor tended to you. In the confusion, the doctors thought there was one Gabriella. My wife died of her injuries from the accident; you were paralyzed and unconscious, but alive. The nurses who cared for both women put my wife's wedding ring on your finger, assuming that it had come off in the confusion. They were very attentive but very rushed and there was not time to manage these details in measure."

Gabriella stared at him. "You are telling me something incomprehensible. You are saying that I, and a woman who looked like me, with the same name, both were brought to the hospital. She died, I lived. Is that it?"

"I saw her grave," Lord Michael said. "She is buried in the plot in the church cemetery where your parents are buried."

Gabriella covered her face with her hands. It was too much to comprehend. Her parents, dead. A stranger buried with them. She should have been in that grave.

She raised stricken blue eyes to meet his compassionate gaze. "How did I survive?"

"No one knows. Your aunt, who knew the house, guesses that you were leaving your bed to go to them when the beam struck you and you fell. A neighbor pulled you to safety and then you were brought to the hospital. My wife was already there. In the confusion, your identity and that of my wife were mingled. She died and was sent to the churchyard for burial with your parents. It must have been a catastrophic time for the hospital staff; I have no doubt that they managed as best they could."

"But that does not suffice to answer the more immediate question: how could your wife and I both look alike, and both have the same name? Such a coincidence cannot be."

"It is not a coincidence," he answered as he took her hands in his. This was the information that, perhaps more than the death of her parents, would test Gabby's strength. "I spoke at length with your aunt. She is a very kind woman with a great devotion to you and to your family. I have not divulged your circumstances; she assumes that it is you who is buried in the church cemetery. Because of that, and because of her grief, she spoke freely."

Gabriella looked at him in dismay. "You sound as if you are about to tell me something unpleasant, something even worse than what I have already learned."

"I hope that you will not regard it as unpleasant. It merely is the truth. You and my wife were sisters, born to a woman in the hospital where your mother was a nurse. Your mother and father had been married for some time and had not been blessed with children. The mother, who was in a very weakened state, delivered twin girls. She then died shortly after the daughters were born. You were the weaker one; your mother felt that you would not survive in a foundling home, which is where your sister was to be taken. She took you home and she and your father raised you as their own. She gave you the name of your dead mother, Gabriella. Your aunt knew the truth and felt that Mrs. Burchell, the mother who raised you, had done the right thing. Your twin sister, my wife, was taken to the foundling home; she was also given the name of the mother who had died. When Gabriella was seventeen, she found employment as a companion to an heiress. I met her and I fell in love and married her. But I soon discovered that her love was an illusion. She was cruel and selfish."

"Perhaps she was so because she was not raised by loving parents," Gabriella cried out. "Perhaps her nature was the result of the circumstances in which she was raised.'

"Perhaps," Lord Michael bowed his head. "I cannot say. I wanted to love her but she did not want my heart. She sought, I suppose, those things that she had lacked growing up in the foundling home: jewels, dresses, adoration . . . she neglected the children she bore, perhaps, you would say, because she had not been given affection in her own childhood. I cannot dispute this. All I know is that you have become part of this household in a way that she never has. The servants who feared her are loyal to you. My children cherish their time with you; their mother regarded them as an encumbrance. I have discovered that it is your sister who is the stranger, and you, Gabby, who are the true mother, the true Duchess. I can only ask you this: will you do me the great honor of becoming my true wife? I vow that I will love you and care for you as I intended to do for her."

"I wanted to marry," she told him, bewildered by his words, "but my mother needed me to care for her. I thought that I would never have children or a husband. You offer me all that I ever wanted. I . . . there will be so much to understand and explain."

"We can tell all in time, at the right time. For now, who need know but the few necessary? Dr. Avery knows because I told him; I trust him implicitly. We can tell your Aunt Ida. Perhaps she would like to come to Lancashire and live here with us. The children must know before we wed, of course. And when the time is right we shall explain to all how the new Duchess of Lancashire has come to be so content to rusticate in the country rather than join the parties and routs in London. Can you love me, do you think? I have been arrogant and demanding, I know," he said, taking her hands and raising them to his lips. "But you have taught me much in these weeks and I know now that it is you that I love."

She studied him. She had been dreading the thought of leaving Wibberley Hall; now she knew that the reason was because she did not want to leave him or the children. What a marvel it was to love where she thought she had despised, and to find her identity in such a labyrinthine set of circumstances.

"I believe that I love you already," she said slowly, absorbing the truth of her love for him.

His lips left her hands and found her mouth, willing and eager for his kiss, but innocent with a love that was his alone. His arms enveloped her in an embrace that said what words could not, that he wanted to protect her from the harm she had suffered and the uncertainty of the past weeks. The glistening snow reflected the streaming sunlight through the window illuminating this Christmas kiss.

As her arms reached out to enfold him, Gabby realized that she was no longer a stranger in this household. She would be a wife and mother, and she was beloved.

Lord Michael pulled away from the kiss gently. "One last thing. You said you chose a present for me as well?"

Gabriella smiled. "The gift you have given me today will make it pale in comparison. But I'm sure I can work out an even better gift for you next Christmas."

EPILOGUE

Gabriella's gift the following Christmas was indeed more than either of them could have imagined. But much happened in the year before it could be given.

Shortly after Gabriella and Lord Michael had declared their love for each other, they had sat both children down and explained what had happened to their real mother. Neither child shed many tears for the distant woman they hardly knew, when their new mother was so loving and kind. With both of the children's blessings, which Gabriella insisted they get before making any plans on marriage, Lord Michael and Gabriella were married in the twilight of the winter season. It was a small wedding, with close family friends there, Dr. Avery, Bessie and Aunt Ida were all intendance. Aunt Ida even came to live closer in a small cottage Lord Michael procured for her.

Gabriella's legs grew strong again, and soon she could walk, run, and play with the children outdoors. She never stopped being grateful for all that she had, even with all that she had lost.

Not long after their wedding, the new Duchess Gabriella had some very exciting news.

On Christmas day, a whole year after both Gabriella's and Lord Michael's lives changed, little Jackson was born.

Lord Michael had to admit, Gabriella really had worked out an even better Christmas gift. A gift so perfect, only God Himself could have given it.

THANK YOU FOR CHOOSING A PUREREAD BOOK!

We hope you enjoyed the story, and as a way to thank you for choosing PureRead we'd like to send you this free book, and other fun reader rewards...

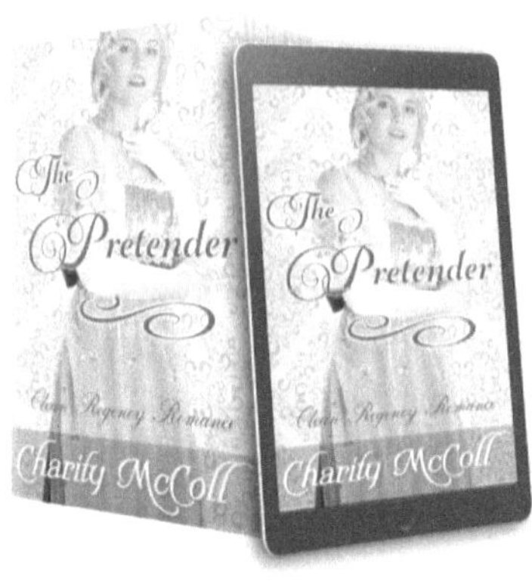

An undercover plan designed to win a young nobleman's heart is threatened when the lovely Gabrielle Belgrade's soft conscience and honesty threatens to undo the matchmaking shenanigans of Lord Grant's well intentioned godmother.

Click here for your free copy of The Pretender
PureRead.com/regency

Thanks again for reading.
See you soon!

AND THERE'S MORE…

We also want to bless you with a first chapter of another brand new Christmas Victorian Romance, Workhouse Girl's Christmas Dream by Rosie Swan. All of our books are clean and wholesome reads, full of strong characters, powerful love, and enduring hope!

Turn the page and let's begin...

WORKHOUSE GIRL'S CHRISTMAS DREAM

PART 1 - CHRISTMAS STORMS

Christmas Day, Walsall County, England.

The storm that had been threatening for days reached the mining village of Walsall when least expected.

Its violence was particularly felt in the old farmhouse that stood next to the village crossroads early in the morning on Christmas Day. A clap of thunder as loud as a blast from the dynamite used in the coal miles rumbled across the house, shaking its very foundations. A bolt of lightning sliced through the sky and struck a tree out in the yard, which immediately burst into flames. It seemed as if nature itself were sending out an ominous sign to the inhabitants of the old farmhouse that morning.

The flaming tree frightened the little girl whose face was pressed to the window as she watched nature in all her glory. She jumped back and crouched under the window sill like a scared rabbit, her eyes wide and filled with terror. In her whole life she'd never seen something as fascinating or as frightening as lightning striking a tree and causing it to burst into flames. That was the tree that she and her parents liked to sit under in the summer, sipping lemonade and watching as the villagers went past. Once in a while villagers would stop and be offered a glass of lemonade to refresh their thirsty throats. Now there would be no more reposing under the tree, and smoke from the burning tree filled the house, causing the child to choke.

For many years to come, eleven-year-old Amanda Jane Wood would always associate Christmas Day with terrible storms, fire, smoke and fear. First, fear of the terrible storm that was raging outside and then also the dark shadow of death that hovered in the three-roomed farmhouse. She coughed and tried to cover her face but in vain; the smoke was thick in the small living room.

Rain blew into the house through one of the cracked windows, soaking the child as she cowered under the windowsill. She rushed out of the living room and went to find her mother who was in her bedchamber. Mandy knew that when her parents' door was closed she wasn't supposed to open it without knocking first. And even then, she had to wait until she was bid to enter, so she stood there with her small hand raised as she prepared to knock. The storm made it impossible for her to hear whatever was going on and she knocked softly then waited.

Mrs. Edna Wood had just finished giving her husband a bed bath and dressing him in his best clothes as a way of preparing him for what was to come. Husband and wife both knew that this day wasn't going to end happily as most Christmas Days in the past had. That was the reason the twenty-nine-year-old man had held onto his wife's hand for a long while. The storm raged on outside, but in this small cosy room two souls were bidding farewell to each other, even though neither wanted to let go.

"Promise me that you'll always take care of Mandy," he whispered, his voice raspy even as his chest heaved. He was struggling to breathe, and she wished he would reserve his strength because talking was taking its toll on him. His once-ruddy skin was now sallow, and she could see the veins on his scrawny hands. Her once-virile man, the champion of her heart, was now nothing but skin and bones. Her heart was breaking, but she put on a brave smile. "And promise me that you'll also take good care of yourself."

"I promise," her voice was also a whisper as she fought back her tears. She had wept in private for many days, and this wasn't the time to do it openly. She had to be strong even though all she wanted to do was raise her head and scream, and ask why this was happening to her happy family. Why did death have to come to one so young when there were many old people in the village, she asked silently, then repented for her wicked thoughts. God was the giver of life and He chose who to preserve and who to take away. It wasn't up to her to decide because she was just a mere human being. But it hurt to know that this was the last time she was going to be with this man who held her heart.

"And always tell her that I love her so much but I have to leave. It's time for me to go, even though I wish I could stay with her, with you, my darling." And his shaking hand brought her palm to his cracked lips where he placed a soft kiss. His face was lined with the fatigue that comes to one who has been ailing for a while and whose body is giving up the fight. "It was so good with you, Edna," he whispered as he let her hand drop, his own too weak to continue holding it, and he closed his eyes. He opened his eyes briefly and smiled, "If I had to do it again, I would choose you over every other woman in the world. I would love you and be with you; always remember that."

The woman nodded, and when he fell asleep, she gazed at the face of the man she had loved for nearly twelve years, and tears coursed down her cheek. Why was death so cruel? And what would happen to her and Mandy when her beloved was gone?

She wiped her eyes because she didn't want Mandy to see her tears and rose up to go and empty the small basin. That's when she met with Mandy at the door of the bedchamber and the child looked terrified.

"Mandy, what's frightened you like this?" She looked toward the living room which was filled with smoke. "And why is there so much smoke in the house? Have you been burning things again?" Her voice was unusually harsh; then she toned it down. "Mandy you know that I've always told you to be careful with fire."

"Mama, the tree in the yard is burning and then the rain is pouring into the living room," Amanda was shivering but whether from the cold or fear or both wasn't clear. "The lightning struck the tree and it started burning."

"I'll fix the window later," Edna wiped the sweat off her forehead with the corner of her sleeve.

"How is Papa? May I go in and see him now? He promised that he would tell me the Christmas story today, Mama."

Edna gave her daughter a sad smile, "Not now, Mandy," she whispered. "Papa is tired and resting." She was normally a strong woman but taking care of her sick husband for the past one month had taken its toll on her. Slender and of average height, her blue eyes were troubled as they settled on her only child. She didn't want to frighten Mandy, but things weren't looking good for them, and their future was uncertain. She knew that Mr. Wood wasn't going to make it to the evening, and she didn't want to imagine what would happen to them after today. He had been her rock from the moment they had met and she felt like she was falling with no one to hold her.

"Mama today is Christmas Day and Mrs. Fount said we should celebrate it at her house with them. Will we be going there later, and will Papa come with us?" Mandy asked as she followed her mother into the third room of the house which served as both kitchen and Mandy's bedroom. Her mother had partitioned the room with a curtain to separate the child's sleeping area from the side they prepared meals on.

"Indeed it's Christmas Day," Mrs. Wood responded absentmindedly as she stroked the fire in the grate. There was a pot of chicken bones on it from their dinner last evening. She was preparing some broth to feed her husband, even though he'd told her that he wasn't hungry any more.

Mandy looked around the kitchen and frowned slightly, wondering why her mother wasn't preparing the delicious pies that she always did when they were visiting their neighbours. In the past all the families in the village celebrated Christmas together and gathered at the home of anyone who chose to be the host for that particular year. This time it was Mrs. Fount who lived on the west side of them and whose house was much bigger than everyone else's in the village. Her husband was the village constable, and her two daughters Gillian and Alison, who were ten and eight respectively, were Mandy's best friends.

Christmas was always such a fun-filled and happy season, but Mandy had the strange feeling that it wasn't going to be like that this year.

"Ma?" Mandy saw the sadness on her mother's face.

"Yes my love?"

"You haven't baked anything to take to Mrs. Fount's house. Will we not have Christmas this year?"

Mrs. Wood sighed as she turned to her daughter. Now was the time for the truth which couldn't be hidden any longer.

"Mandy, you'll soon be twelve and are growing up, and I don't want to hide anything from you any longer."

Mandy felt fear but looked at her mother with wide eyes, hazel like her father's.

"You know that your father has been very ill this past one month and we were hoping he would get better. Sadly, that hasn't been the case, so all the money we had has been used up in getting him medicines. There's nothing left for me to buy even half a pound of ham to make pies, and we have no flour in the bin," She smiled and pulled Mandy close. "But I promise you that next year things will be better."

"So Papa will get better and then we'll have a good Christmas next year, Ma?"

"Oh Mandy," Edna had prayed for that miracle from the moment her husband had noticed the blood in his sputum when he coughed. That had been two months ago and she had done all she could, using all the traditional remedies she remembered her mother teaching her. From warm milk laced with honey, to boiled roots, there was nothing she hadn't tried. But the cough had only gotten worse and finally they had to accept the truth.

Mandy and her mother held each other for a while listening as the storm began to abate. As the storm died down, a heavy bout of coughing from the bedchamber made her mother immediately release her. She ran out of the kitchen.

Mandy wanted to follow her, but something held her back. She hated seeing her father suffering and especially when he tried to pretend he wasn't in pain. Her mother had told her that she shouldn't tire him by asking too many questions. She also didn't want to go back to the living room which was chilly and full of smoke. Her stomach rumbled with hunger and she wished her mother would serve her some of the broth that was bubbling merrily on the fire.

Mama would take care of things once she was done taking care of Papa, the child thought as she moved behind the curtain to her small cot. She climbed on it and curled up, feeling the warmth from her frayed blanket. Papa had promised to buy her a nice woollen one once he got better and she smiled at the thought.

Mandy never complained even when she went without a lot of the things that Jill and Ally possessed. She always believed that one day her father would buy her everything her heart desired, and so her life was filled with childish contentment.

Jill and Ally had a large bedroom in which they slept but Mandy loved her spot here in the kitchen. She always lay on her small bed and watched her mother cooking, most times falling asleep because of the warmth from the fire and having to be woken up to eat.

Her eyes felt heavy even as she listened to the murmuring voices in the other room. Her parents were probably talking about what to do for Christmas and she smiled as she closed her eyes. The little girl was soon asleep, unaware that life was about to change for them forever.

It was the wailing that roused Mandy from her deep sleep. At first she thought it was part of the dream she'd been having. But then she became aware of footsteps coming and going in the kitchen which had earlier been empty. And she could smell something besides the chicken broth that had been boiling on the fire. Pie and freshly baked bread!

The little girl's stomach growled again and she pushed the curtain aside and got off her narrow cot, wondering if her mother had been fibbing before. A smile broke out on her face as she saw the small kitchen table. It was loaded with many covered dishes emitting delicious aromas. Yes, Christmas Day was going to be a celebration and it was being held at their house.

"I must be dreaming," the child thought because just before she'd fallen asleep there had been nothing in the kitchen. Yet now the small table was groaning under the weight of all the dishes placed upon it. No one seemed to have noticed her yet so she reached out a hand to pick up a pie from the tray nearest to her bed. Mama wouldn't mind and besides, she was so hungry. She'd just taken the first bite out of the fruit pie when the loud wail came again and the small sweet pastry dropped from her hand to the floor.

"Mama," Mandy cried out, recognising the wailing voice and rushing out of the kitchen, brushing past neighbours who moved out of the way for her. Her mother was in her bedchamber and Mrs. Fount and Mrs. Wiser another neighbour were seated on the bed on either side of her mother.

Mandy frowned because this room was her parents' private domain and she couldn't recall any time that neighbours had been allowed inside. And yet here they were and she couldn't see any signs of her father who was supposed to be in the bed that her mother and the neighbours were sitting on.

"Ma?" Mandy stood at the doorway, too scared to go into her parents' bedchamber. That her mother was crying and wailing clearly meant that something bad had happened. The only other time she'd seen her mother this upset was years ago when she was about four and her grandmother and grandfather had died just days apart from each other. And on that day Mandy had seen her father wrapping his arms around her mother and comforting her. But if something bad had happened, where was her father to comfort her mother again?

"Oh, Mandy," her mother caught sight of her and held her arms out. Mandy ran to her mother and fell into her arms. "Oh, Mandy," she repeated, tears clogging her throat.

Mandy suddenly got the feeling that she was never going to see her father again. At eleven years of age the young girl knew about death after losing both sets of grandparents when she was of an age of reasoning. And also, they lived in a mining village where they had one or two funerals a week. Though she was still too young to comprehend the effects of coal mining on the lives of the miners, she knew that people who worked in the mines were always dying; then they were buried and their families mourned.

When her grandparents had died, she and her mother had been comforted by her father. But he wasn't here now, and she'd never once thought that she would be one of those children in the village who lost their fathers. A few of her friends had buried their fathers, but Mandy always thought that such a misfortune was far from her. Now a red cord would be stuck to the front of their door, signifying that the angel of death had visited them, as her father liked to say.

"Papa?" She asked softly and her mother heard her. This had to be a bad dream and she willed herself to wake up.

"Mandy, we have to be strong. Your father has gone and left us," Mrs. Wood broke into sobbing even as her arms tightened around her daughter. "What will I do now without you, Anthony," the woman wailed.

"We're here for you and your daughter," Mrs. Fount put her arms around Mandy and her mother. "My family will help in every way that we can," she made the promise, which Mandy was to remember at a later date.

"Death comes to all of us at one time or other," Mrs. Wiser said, confirming Mandy's fears. Her father was dead and she knew that he would soon be put in a hole in the ground like all the other dead people she'd seen; they would cover him with earth and she would never see him again.

Then Mandy felt something rising within her, from her stomach it moved to her chest then throat and forced its way out of her in a wail that many would later say had sent chills down their backs.

"No," she struggled to get free of her mother's arms. Mrs. Fount's arms dropped but her mother's held fast. She wanted to be set free so she could go and meet her father at the end of the bridge where she liked to wait for him as he returned from the mines which were about two miles from the village. What her childish mind refused to accept was that the coal mines had claimed yet another victim, and this time it was her father. Anthony Wood, loving husband and beloved father was no more.

"Pa is coming back," the child wailed. "Let me alone so I can go and wait for him at the bridge," she struggled to get free but her mother's arms only tightened around her small body.

"Mandy, you have to be strong," Mrs. Wiser said. "Your mama needs you right now. Stop that nonsense at once and accept what has happened. Denying it won't make your father come back."

But the child ignored the woman's harsh rebuke and continued to struggle in her mother's arms. Finally Mrs. Wood's hands were too weak and tired to continue holding the struggling child and she let go. Mandy rushed out of the room, ignoring calls from the neighbours who seemed to be everywhere. Their small house was filled with people, but she brushed them all aside when they tried to reach for her. She raced through the small living room where she saw Mr. Fount, the police constable who also acted as coroner whenever anyone died, and she also saw Reverend Jones, the vicar of their parish along with a few other male neighbours. They were standing around talking, but she didn't wait to hear what they had to say.

"Mandy," another voice called out as she tore out of the house through the front door, noticing the red cord hanging from the door. Her eyes were fixed on the road. It had stopped raining and the sun was even trying to break through the thick clouds. Mandy's focus was on getting to the bridge where she would wait for her father and skip beside him all the way home. Usually he left a little bit of whatever her mother had packed for his lunch and gave it to her as a present for waiting for him.

Come rain or sunshine, the child never missed a day waiting for her father at the bridge, unless she was sick and in bed.

There were few people on the road on account of the heavy storm that had passed. And also, it was early afternoon on Christmas Day and most folks were at home taking long lunches or early dinners. But none of Mandy's friends whose fathers also worked in the mines were outside as usual. That didn't even occur to her as she ran on, even though she soon found herself alone on the road.

Usually all the children of Walsall Village whose fathers worked in the coal mines would race each other to Old Walsall Bridge and play there among the rocks until the men arrived. Then each child would walk or dance back home with their father.

Today, however, it didn't occur to Mandy that the road leading to the bridge was empty. Her grief shrouded her in a world of her own, pushing her back into the past and she didn't even remember that it was Christmas Day and the mines were shut down until after the holidays. All she wanted was her father.

Mandy got to the bridge, crossed it and sat down on one of the many little rocks that someone had once called the waiting station. One or two people passed by, giving her odd looks but the child's eyes were fixed on the path that her father usually took from the mines.

"Not my Pa," Mandy muttered as a man hurried toward the bridge and crossed it to the other side. "Not my Pa," she said of yet another, getting into the game she and her friends usually played as they waited. The game would go on until one of the children spotted his or her father. Thereafter, the lucky child would jump up and shout,

"My Pa is here, no more delays, no more waiting," and the others would giggle and continue with the game until the last man had returned. Sometimes when there was an explosion or a cave in at the mines, the children and their mothers would huddle together at the 'waiting station', each praying that their father and husband wasn't the latest victim to be claimed by the mines.

"Mandy," the soft voice broke through the child's continuous muttering and she looked up to find her mother crossing the bridge.

"Ma," she said, "I've been waiting for my Pa, but he isn't here yet. And I haven't seen the other men returning. Are they still working in the mines?" Mandy's eyes returned to the path leading to the mines.

"Oh Mandy," her mother walked slowly towards her. Mandy noted that she looked very tired and her eyes were red. Mrs. Wood had suffered five miscarriages, and when she'd given up hope of ever having a child, Mandy had been conceived.

It was clear to all that the little girl was the apple of her parents' eyes, but rather than become pampered and spoiled, she had such a sweet nature that everyone in the village liked her. The traders and store owners always had little treats for her whenever her parents sent her to get groceries.

"Mandy, today is Christmas Day and the mines are closed for the holidays," her mother reminded gently. She sat down on the same rock as her daughter and stretched out her shawl to cover them both.

Mandy raised stricken eyes to her mother. "Then where is my Pa?"

"Oh, Mandy," Mrs. Wood pulled her daughter close. "It's so cold out here and I need to get you home where it's warm. Besides, we have visitors and shouldn't leave them alone or they will think that we're being very poor hosts."

"But Pa…"

"Mandy!" Her mother's voice was gentle but firm. "For the past one month your father never went to the mines and you know the reason why, don't you? Remember that you haven't been out here to the bridge in all that time," Mrs. Wood raised her daughter's chin. "Your Pa was very sick and he was hurting terribly. You even saw that sometimes he would cough out blood and then wasn't able to breathe properly. He wanted to stay with us but the pain was too much for him to bear," Mrs. Wood's voice broke on a sob. "He begged me to let him go even when I didn't want to, and told me to tell you that he loves you so much and will be watching over you from heaven."

"But he didn't ask me before he left," Mandy cried out. "Why didn't he ask me? I wouldn't have let him go."

"Mandy, your father didn't want you to be sad so he didn't ask you."

"Ma, but why did he leave us? Didn't he love us anymore?" Mandy began to sob. "Why did he find it so easy to leave us?"

"Mandy, he didn't find it easy to leave us because he held on for as long as he could," Mrs. Wood said. Her husband, like many other miners before him, had suffered from black lung disease, which had only worsened as the days went by. "Your Pa loved us both so much but the pain became unbearable, and I let him rest," Mrs. Wood sobbed. The two held each other close and wept together for a long while.

They sat there at the 'waiting station' until the village lamplighter passed over the bridge, his ladder in his hand, on his way to light the gas streetlights.

"We have to get back home," Mandy heard her mother saying as if from a distance. "It's getting dark and we don't want to be out here until late." She rose to her feet and pulled Mandy up. Mother and daughter walked back home hand in hand, stopping every few steps to receive condolence messages from their neighbours.

And everyone had nice things to say about her father. Mandy heard them praising her father and saying that he was a good man who would be greatly missed. She wanted to shout and tell people not to talk about her father as if he wasn't there. Then she remembered that he was gone and actually wasn't there and fresh tears filled her eyes.

She would miss her Pa so much, and it was true: he'd been a very good man. Young as she was, Mandy understood what love was because she'd seen and experienced it in her home. And her father never stopped telling her and her mother that he loved them with his whole heart. Though they didn't have much, no one in need was ever turned away from their door.

"Even if there's nothing to eat in the house, make sure that everyone who comes to our door gets at least a simple glass of water," were her father's words to her so many times.

Mandy never understood why her father was so generous, sometimes causing her mother to complain that he was too kind. But Mr. Wood would simply laugh, ruffle Mandy's hair and kiss his wife's cheek.

"The Apostle Paul tells us to always open our homes to strangers for who knows, we may one day even welcome an angel into our humble abode," he would say. "And always remember that…"

"Angels are messengers who bring blessings from God to His people," Mandy and her mother would finish his sentence and they would all laugh.

It was because of her father's example that Mandy had learned to share everything she had with her friends. But sometimes they weren't as giving as she was, and she would then get upset and complain to her father.

"Mandy, don't always expect to be repaid for your kindness and generosity," he'd once told her when Jill and Ally refused to share their pastries with her. She had complained to him that her friends were very mean and yet she always shared everything with them. "Just do good, and one day it will find you when you need it most. God always rewards generosity even if it isn't immediately. What you hand out to someone through the front door returns to you through the back door."

Mrs. Wood paused at their small gate and Mandy looked up to see that someone had already lit the lanterns in the house and even placed two on the small porch. Their house was brighter than usual and she could see the red cord hanging on the open door. She wanted to rush up and tear it down.

Their small living room was filled with people and as soon as Mandy and her mother entered the house, the mourners parted to let them through. And that was when Mandy saw her father lying on the bier, covered up to his neck with a white sheet. He looked so peaceful and it was as if his lips were about to burst into a smile like they always did. Her Pa was such a happy man and she couldn't remember ever seeing him sad.

There was silence in the house as everyone watched to see what the child would do. They had seen her running out before and were worried that she wasn't in a very good frame of mind.

Mandy approached the bier, "My Pa looks like he's sleeping," she spoke to no one in particular. Mr. Anthony Wood looked peaceful in death, just as he had in life. "I wish he would open his eyes and wake up," she murmured.

She stood beside the bier for a long time, not feeling afraid of the dead body as was her usual practice. Even when a neighbour died and her parents took her to pay their respects to the family, Mandy would never get close to the bier.

Yet now she drew close without any fear, putting out a hand to touch her father's cold face. "Pa is cold," Mandy said, adjusting the bed sheet. A sob broke out among the mourners but Mandy ignored it. "I wish he was still here with us," she said sadly.

Then she turned to find her mother watching her. So she walked to where she was and put her arms around her.

"Ma, please don't ever go away like Pa and leave me alone."

Mrs. Wood choked up, "Oh, Mandy!"

"Now what will we do without my Pa," the child asked in a soft voice, sounding very lost.

· · ·

What will happen to Mandy and her mother?

Workhouse Girl's Christmas Dream is a heartbreakingly beautiful Christmas story of rags to riches set in Victorian England. Mandy's story is one you will enjoy to the final happy ever after…

Continue Reading on Amazon

Continue Reading on Amazon

OUR GIFT TO YOU

AS A WAY TO SAY THANK YOU WE WOULD LOVE TO SEND YOU THIS BEAUTIFUL STORY FREE OF CHARGE.

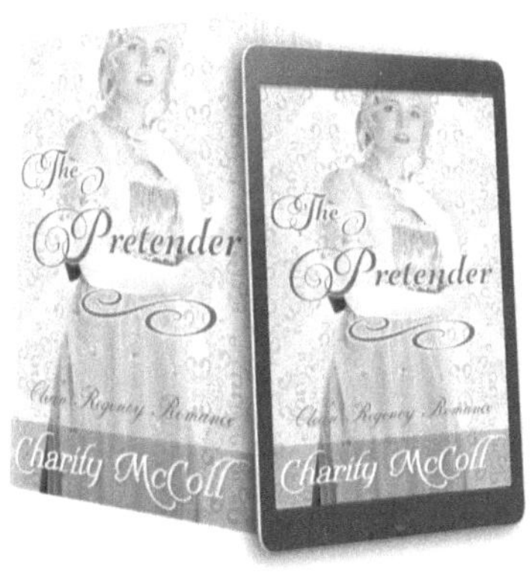

An undercover plan designed to win a young nobleman's heart is threatened when the lovely Gabrielle Belgrade's soft conscience and honesty threatens to undo the matchmaking shenanigans of Lord Grant's well intentioned godmother.

Click here for your free copy of The Pretender

PureRead.com/regency

At PureRead we publish books you can trust. Great tales without smut or swearing, but with all of the mystery and romance you expect from a great story.

Be the first to know when we release new books, take part in our fun competitions, and get surprise free books in your inbox by signing up to our free VIP Reader list.

As a thank you you'll receive a copy of *The Pretender* straight away in you inbox.

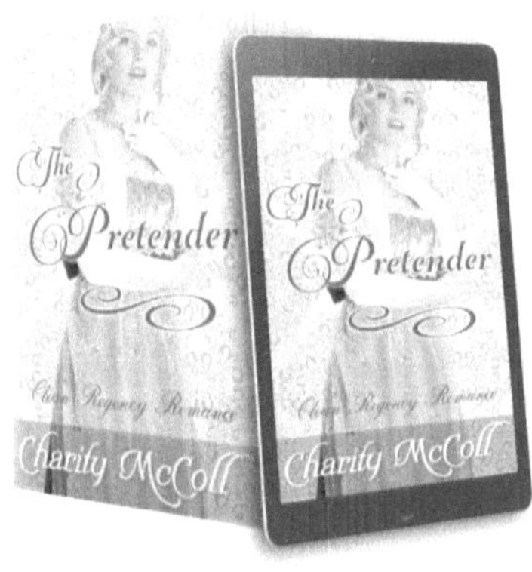

Click here for your free copy of The Pretender

PureRead.com/regency